SHADOWSCAPE
The Stevie Vegas Chronicles

By
M. R. WESTON

This book is dedicated to my three sons Erad, Jack & Callum. There's no place like home...

Table of Contents

PROLOGUE

I haven't written in this diary for a long, long time. A year, maybe two but it seems like a lifetime ago now...when I was just a kid. I'd really like to go back to that time, before it all started. Things were simple then...

Then the biggest thing I ever got up to was a dare to run through McShady's motor wrecking yard at a hundred kilometres an hour while he slept in his old timber shed, and before he called the cops. That was before I moved to Smithson with my folks, before I heard of Extra Sensory Perception (ESP) and discovered my talent for making things happen.

Some would say I was getting even with the people that wronged me and my family...when the *accident* happened. Getting even with the people that hurt my brother Jem and caused my world to come crashing down. Evening the score with the Barrons. But they didn't know about It. Yeah, It, the power that changed my life forever. It's a curse and a power that I still don't understand, much less control.

I remember when I was 10 years old and I remember my old life in Valley Dale. Dad and mum were happy then - we were a normal family, looked up to and even and admired. Now I'm just known as the weird boy who was somehow to blame for Jacob Barron's *accident*. Why? Why did we have to move to Smithson - a little black hole of a place in the middle of nowhere, with an evil centre that's rotten to the core?

Some people would say I was in the wrong place at the wrong time. I can't disagree with that. You see now that I know what I know, I wish I didn't know it and to be honest, I'm not sure how to get past that. I can't forget what I know...or what I've seen. It's no coincidence. It can't be.

Life's strange and this power I've got, that I sure as hell don't want, makes me a little bit stranger.

This will be my last entry for a while, though it helps to write it all down. I really need to figure this thing out in my head and make sense of what's happened. The only way I can do that is to stop running and face It.

I can hear the thoughts again, like soft voices in the wind. I know its Jacob Barron's family cursing the day we ever came to town. And I can hear my mum's thoughts...she's sad and wishing for Valley Dale too.

And I can hear him - Jacob Barron - his voice, far off, like he is talking to someone, or something.

He can't be. He's in a coma and the doctors say he'll never recover. But that's not what I'm hearing.

He's making a deal with someone to get well again. Someone all powerful and I know it's not God. Their voices are menacing and dark, like they come from the other side of a veil, a dark veil that no-one would ever want to see through.

But my strange powers have opened a doorway through to this world and, like it or not, I've got to learn how to survive in this evil mindscape.

I wish I was back in McShady's wrecking yard where the only thing I had to fear was buckshot in my backside and a ride home in the police car. Now, I have to fear for my life.

CHAPTER 1 - SKATING AND JEM

Stevie Vegas executed a pretty good Grind on the metal railing of the stairs leading down to Hill St. With a smile on his face that said he was supremely pleased with his skateboarding form, he flicked his board in the air and caught it neatly.

Crossing the road he just about ran the rest of the way home, aware he was very late for breakfast. He knew without even knowing that his mum would be uptight. He was an hour late and he had promised her one thing that morning as he not only pleaded to go skating before school, but after school as well. He knew he was pushing his luck, but turned up the charm: "I'll be home in time for tea. Just an hour before and after school at the skate park - I swear two hours max."

As he sat down to breakfast, late as usual, he knew he would have to do some serious begging to be allowed out again to the skate park this afternoon. "Since when have you noticed the time," his mum said in a semi-stern voice, with just a hint of a smile.

She was stirring his porridge on the stove, but he knew without looking that she wasn't really angry or disappointed with him, just a little annoyed with a son whose passion for skateboarding often made him forget the important things - like eating.

Stevie pushed the long fringe that mostly hung over his left eye away so that his mum could see his sky blue...and innocent eyes. "Please, mum. I promise." he said, his voice full of the tone that said this was something he really, really wanted.

Mrs Vegas turned from the stove to her son, the smile gone from her face.

"Stevie you and I know the trouble you and your brother were in last month. Goodness poor old Ian McShady was scared out of wits, and you both could have been hurt. What were you thinking sneaking out at night and running through his yard?"

He looked down at the porridge placed in front of him. It had little pieces of apple and a big dollop of honey sitting on top, just ready to be stirred through. It reminded him just how much his mum did for him and his brother Jem.

Stevie stirred his porridge. Maybe he would leave skateboarding after all and catch a walk home with Jem instead. Kicking a soccer ball round the backyard was, after all, not too dreary. And then there was the matter of McShady's yard. He had a bit of making up to do.

Maybe he should give the skate park a miss. He was just about to tell his mum that when he noticed an easing of the tension that hung in the air. "OK," his mum said. "One hour at the park this afternoon and that's it. And I want you in full protective gear. Right?"

Stevie nodded and smiled at her enthusiastically. "You are the best," he said, giving his mum a big hug before grabbing his bag and board and running out the door. The school bus was just pulling into the kerb.

"I'll be home before tea," he promised, waving goodbye.

Stevie Vegas was by and large a good kid. He was mature for his 12 years, the kind of maturity that adults noticed. His quiet, essentially shy demeanor hid a budding talent for getting it right about people. He had the uncanny ability to "read" people. Even he wasn't sure how he did it - but he just knew. Knew the milkman was a thief who was about to rifle through his mum's bag when she went to pick up the empty milk bottles from the laundry, and knew that his grandma was about to pass away the night before his mum took the phone call from his aunt Jackie in Lilydale.

But that wasn't all. Stevie Vegas could also read minds.

8

He didn't know yet that's what he could do - only sensed he was different from the rest and that difference sometimes made him, and other people, uncomfortable. That might have explained why he went to the extreme in some things - like skateboarding and what he wore and how he looked. Black jeans, black T-shirts and his brown hair with a fringe that hung over his face, partly obscuring his piercing blue eyes that were the most remarkable feature on his face.

The last thing Stevie Vegas wanted to do was become too noticeable. Keeping it simple and staying in the background meant that he didn't have to show the surprise on his face when he "heard" his next door neighbour thinking about leaving his family for a better life while talking to his mum about the weather. Or how he knew his mum was thinking about telling his father to slow down a minute before the policeman pulled his dad over for speeding. Stevie also knew that the policeman would be just up a head waiting for his dad too.

He'd given up telling anyone that he knew what they were thinking because he'd grown tired of that look they gave him - like they knew more than him and that he was just some silly kid. Reading people's minds was...well it was crazy and impossible. These days he kept his thoughts, as well as his warnings, to himself. Only, knowing things the way he did came in handy at times.

Like the time he rescued Jem from the schoolyard bullies. It happened in Phys Ed. They had Jem trussed up like a chicken with a bit of rope the caretaker had left under the stairs. Before the teacher had left the class for five minutes, the bullies had already identified their next victim - Jem.

Jem was short for his age. At 11 he was considered a small kid and he was also a slim build. His size was handy on the soccer field 'because he was fast, but in the schoolyard he was easy prey. As soon as the teacher left the room they tackled him and despite his protests trussed him up and had him down on the ground, and were about to lay the boot in to him. That was, until Stevie came shooting through the door with the school's loud speaker.

"One more move...," he yelled, turning the amplifier up as loud as it would go. "You scumbags leave Jem Vegas alone or I'll find you one by one on a dark night...and you won't know I'm coming." He raised his voice to a deep shout. "Now *do* you understand me!"

They all stood absolutely still for a moment, shocked by Stevie's appearance. After all, Stevie Vegas hardly every spoke to anyone except his brother Jem and here he was unleashing his very loud voice over the school's loudspeaker. One of the bullies attempted to shut him up, but Stevie was having none of that. He repeated his threat again, only louder this time and staring them all straight in the eye.

At the precise moment he finished yelling through the loudspeaker, a clatter caught the group's attention. Just behind them a bag of gym equipment - baseballs, bats and soccer balls - toppled over, sending their contents hurtling towards the bullies. In the midst of all the noise, as the boys dodged the rolling balls, Stevie caught Jem's eye and gave him a wink. Jem managed a weak smile - only he knew what his brother was capable of doing with his extraordinary powers. Unfortunately the bullies had no idea who they were dealing with.

Despite the confusion and the rolling balls, for one moment the leader of the pack thought about taking Stevie Vegas on but decided against it. Stevie was a quiet boy, but there was also something a bit unusual about him. Did he make the gym bag fall - the bully couldn't be sure but he did know that Stevie Vegas was an unknown quantity, and the bully wasn't stupid. He could sense a hidden power within Stevie. Without knowing what it was, like all cowards, he didn't want to test something he wasn't sure about. And he wasn't sure now that Stevie Vegas was such an easy mark. Actually he had a growing doubt in his mind that Jem also wasn't an easy mark when he had a brother like Stevie.

The ringleader stammered: "Eh, ease off. We were only mucking about."

Stevie put down the loudspeaker and flicked his long fringe out of his eyes, staring straight at them. "Untie him or I start yelling again and Mr Binns is just up the corridor - within 10 seconds he'll be back in here."

"Maybe I'll start counting....one, two, three..." Stevie said, stepping menacingly closer.

The small blonde haired boy that hung around sometimes with the bullies was the first to move and he could sense the ringleader had given up the fight. "Alright," the ringleader said. "Chill out Vegas, we didn't mean any harm." He bent down and untied Jem.

"Four, five, six..." Stevie continued.

They half pushed Jem over to Stevie, like a stolen package they'd got caught with. "Here, if you want him, take him. Anyway, you two are dead meat next time I see you," the ringleader said.

Stevie pushed Jem behind him, stood his ground and kept counting. "Nine, ten."

On the count of ten the classroom door opened and there was Mr Binns. The bullies stared at Stevie Vegas, mouths open and disbelief in their eyes.

Stevie winked back at the bullies and then quietly turned to face the teacher. "Sorry sir," he said innocently. "I just needed to give my brother Jem a message from mum. Err...thanks, I'll be getting back to science class now...thanks..." With that, he sped off, leaving everyone, including Jem, staring after him.

It was this same sense of bravery that got him through his front door that night knowing that he was an hour late for tea and would have to face the scariest person in the world. His mum.

CHAPTER 2 - THERE'S NO PLACE LIKE HOME

The Vegas family had lived in suburban Hill St, Valley Dale, for 10 years - long enough for it to be the only home Stevie could remember.

Alexander and Sylvia Vegas were the town's vets. In fact the Vegas home resembled a small zoo. If a sick animal needed a human touch in the night, they were brought home and put in front of the Vegas' fire. Sometimes, if it was possible, Stevie's parents would let the sick animal sleep with either Stevie or Jem. That's of course when Jem wasn't sleeping in Stevie's spare bunk.

"Come on," Jem would say to Stevie. "I promise I'll be quiet. Can't I just *sit* on your spare bed?" Inevitably Stevie would relent and within the hour Jem would be snoring his head off while Stevie was trying to finish his homework. That was the thing about Jem, he could fall asleep anywhere - standing up if he had too.

Whenever he could Jem would follow Stevie around. Most of the time, Stevie didn't much care about the following. He had a strong feeling he should protect Jem. At least that's how he felt when Jem wasn't annoying him.

With vets for parents both boys grew up around animals, learning the subtle art of communicating with animals of all persuasions, from puppies to snakes. Once Stevie's dad even brought home a baby bear!

Both boys learned early in their lives that to care for something so fragile and to contribute to making it well again, delivered a happiness and satisfaction like no other. To watch the dull light in a little puppy's eyes grow stronger and brighter through a bit of love and lots of hard work, generally in the middle of the night, taught the Vegas boys more about life than any science or English class could.

As a result of their upbringing, both boys grew sensitive to the feelings of others. Without really knowing why, they anticipated what people might say. And they could certainly read each other's thoughts. It was uncanny to see them. Their parents would watch their boys, not thinking that anything was unusual, and delighted their boys were so close. But it was more than closeness. Stevie and Jem Vegas were blood brothers of the closest kind. They knew what the other was thinking and when they were apart they could sense or "see" what was happening to the other, particularly in times of danger.

That was how Stevie made it to the gym that day when the bullies trussed Jem. He was in English class listening to Mrs Baker's lecture on how to write an essay, when he saw in his mind's eye, as clearly as a photograph, Jem tied and gagged, laying on the ground. As the image of Jem faded the cruel face of the ringleader came into focus.

But that was one of many events Stevie couldn't explain and he'd given up trying to figure out why, when he saw things or "heard" thoughts, it always turned out he was right.

Stevie knew that night as he pushed his front door open; skateboard in hand, that he would cop a tongue lashing from his mum. He didn't need to be a mind reader to know that was coming.

"Stevie Vegas, is that you?" his mum yelled down the hallway. "You are an hour late. You promised to leave that skate park on time. You are absolutely grounded for one week."

Before Stevie even got to the dinner table he knew he'd be going nowhere for a week and perfecting that Ollie he'd been practicing on his skateboard would have to wait.

But that wasn't what caught his attention.

Sitting in the living room next to his dad was a middle aged man - nothing unremarkable about that - except for the black shadow that seemed to silhouette the stranger. The shadow seemed to grow darkest around the man's head, like a deathly halo.

It was enough to make Stevie stop mid step. He had never seen anything like it. Over the years he had become used to "hearing" other people's thoughts, but never...not once had he ever seen anything like this. He blinked and shook his head from side to side, as if to erase the trick the light must surely be playing on his eyes. He must have looked quite silly standing there gawping at the man. Luckily his father's good manners broke the silence as he eagerly introduced the stranger to his son.

"Stevie this is Chris Barron, the Mayor of Smithson. Mr Barron this is my eldest son Stevie," Mr Vegas said.

Stevie reluctantly extended his hand to Mr Barron, not at all sure what was going to happen given the dark, swirling shadow followed Mr Barron when he got up from the couch to shake Stevie's hand. He looked quickly to his father, hoping that he too saw the wafting, black vapor. His father appeared not to notice, oblivious to everything but the apparent charm of Mr Barron who was smiling engagingly at Stevie.

"Very pleased to meet you Stevie Vegas," Mr Barron said, grasping his hand so firmly that the thought crossed Stevie's mind that his touch was slightly menacing. It was then that the strangest thing happened. As Mr Barron began shaking his hand, Stevie felt the room begin to blur, as though he was being sucked into the heart of a black vortex. The lights dimmed, like they do sometimes before a power surge and he began to feel sick to the stomach. He didn't know why but when he looked at the black vapor, it began to grow, completely surrounding Mr Barron.

Fear replaced the sick feeling in his stomach and he knew instinctively he did not want to be in the same room as this man. Before he could pull his hand away Stevie heard the words: "There is something special about this boy."

Trying desperately not to show his growing panic Stevie withdrew his hand quickly, noticing a slightly puzzled expression cross Mr Barron's face.

"Uh, I might just go and wash up before dinner...," Stevie muttered, trying not to look Mr Barron in the eyes. Instead he locked his gaze with his dad's, as if giving him a silent cue that it was his turn to talk and break the uncomfortable silence that was developing.

"Right," Mr Vegas said. "But be quick. Your mum has been waiting to serve out dinner and you know you are late."

Stevie heaved a sigh of relief and quickly took his cue to leave the room, starting for the stairs almost at a run. He couldn't be rid of this room and this man quick enough.

"And Stevie, Mr Barron will be joining us for tea," his father called after him.

Stevie took the stairs two and a time, practically running to the sanctuary of his own room. He had never experienced a situation like the one that had just occurred downstairs and he was trying his best to process it. The strange feeling in his stomach began to subside as soon as he shut his bedroom door. He leaned against it and closed his eyes, conscious that his breathing was shallow and quick.

What was this man doing in his house? The Vegas home had always been a happy, warm place, yet within the space of a few minutes, this stranger had changed all that with his mere presence. Even now Stevie could feel the chill wind creeping up the stairs. He didn't know why but he felt a nagging unease and began chewing his bottom lip - a habit left over from preschool years when Jem locked him in the cupboard and lost the keys. He'd been two hours in the darkness and as a result had developed a nervous habit. Whenever he was nervous or facing an unknown of any kind he began to chew his lip - a sure sign he definitely didn't feel in control.

But as worried as he was beginning to feel, he was also determined to find out who Mr Barron was. Whether his father had noticed or not, Stevie sensed darkness within Mr Barron that he had never seen or felt so strongly in any other human being. And he wasn't fooled by the man's charm either. He had seen the dark aura and whatever Mr Barron meant by "he's special", Stevie sensed it wasn't good.

CHAPTER 3 - THE PROPOSITION

Stevie took in the scene as he descended the stairs slowly, one at a time and not his usual three steps at a time. He also didn't finish with a star jump off the last four. No, not tonight, not with that threatening stranger a mere 10 metres away.

His mum was serving a generous helping of the beef casserole she had prepared that afternoon onto Mr Barron's plate while his dad filled his glass with red wine. Jem was talking excitedly to Mr Barron, his usually calm, passive face alive with animation, and something else...admiration.

The scene was like something out of their family Christmas album. Why were they being so friendly to this stranger? Stevie stared intently at Mr Barron, approaching the table with caution in each step, hoping not to see the dark shadow again - thinking that it had been the lights in the lounge room before, or perhaps he was overtired from the double training session that day at the skate park.

Too soon he realised that he had not been mistaken. The shadow was still shrouding the Vegas' dinner guest and he noticed that awful feeling in the pit of his stomach was starting again. He sat down quickly, trying not to look in Mr Barron's direction. But this menacing stranger who had captivated his family - a family clearly oblivious to the danger he presented, did not make it that easy for him to slip to the table unnoticed.

"Why Stevie, I'm glad you are able to join us," Mr Barron said, speaking as if he was the host and that Stevie had done them a favour in sitting down to dinner with them. "I was just telling your brother Jem about the great cricket facilities we have in Smithson." Turning to Mr Vegas, he continued, "Your Jem is quite the up and coming baseball talent I hear."

17

Mr Vegas nodded enthusiastically. If he was proud of anything in life, it was not his thriving vet practice, nor the countless animals he'd saved or even that he was one of the most respected citizens of Valley Dale. No his pride and his weakness were his sons. "Yes...why yes, as a matter of a fact Jem was selected in the representative side last summer. Played against the best in the Regionals."

It was Mr Barron's turn to nod enthusiastically. "That's fantastic," he said, a huge grin on his face. "You have to nurture talent as you well know."

Stevie studied Mr Barron as he was talking to his dad. He guessed Mr Barron was somewhere between 40 and 45 years, but you could never tell with adults once they got past about 35 and before they turned 50. He was almost bald, with a semi-circle of closely cropped black/grey hair around the crown of his head - the kind that made people his age shave their heads and go completely bald in a bid to look younger.

As far as Stevie knew what handsome was, Mr Barron could be called handsome. He had piercing dark brown eyes, that flashed every now and then with something Stevie couldn't put his finger on. Of one thing he was sure, those eyes would flash anger if provoked. But most of all Stevie noticed his magnetism and the fact he held centre stage.

Mr Barron was doing most of the talking around the dinner table and his family was letting him talk non-stop, as if it was his home not theirs. Stevie glanced first at his mum and then at his dad, hoping to catch their eye and draw the conversation away from Mr Barron, but it was as if he wasn't there. The behavior of his family, the whole night so far, perplexed Stevie because few people ever dined with the Vegas' - his mum and dad had a special rule. Dinner time was family time.

Mr Barron turned his penetrating gaze on Stevie. "I hear that Jem is not the only talented one in this family....I hear you have a very special talent." He took a long, slow sip from his glass of wine. Stevie concentrated on the red liquid disappearing into his mouth, trying hard not to look into the swirling mass of shadow behind Mr Barron.

"I...err...don't know what you mean," Stevie asked puzzled. "I don't play baseball and I don't do much sport actually."

"Ah, yes, the talent I've heard about has a lot to do with the agility of the mind and is very special; very special indeed."

"I'm not sure I know what you mean Mr Barron," Stevie replied. He was not quite sure what the stranger was getting at. Did he know Stevie could read minds? Surely not, no-one knew that except his family and they wouldn't have told.

He looked desperately at his parents for help but they had stopped eating and were looking at him expectantly. Even Jem had stopped spooning large quantities of casserole into his mouth. They were all, including Mr Barron, apparently waiting for his reply.

Stevie began chewing the bottom of his lip again. "I'm sorry Mr Barron but I really don't know what you mean - I am not special, nor have I any particular talent for anything."

"Stevie you are far too modest about your abilities....at least the ones you displayed at the skate park this afternoon," Mr Barron said, almost triumphantly. "I stopped there on my way over to visit your parents. You see my son Jacob is also an amateur skater. Smithson has one of the finest skate park facilities for hundreds of kilometres."

Stevie let out a huge sigh of relief and smoothed his fringe so that it wasn't partly obscuring his face. Mr Barron had not been referring to his mindreading, but to his skating.

He looked at Mr Barron in a slightly new light, relaxing just a little. Maybe there was nothing to be suspicious about after all. "Ah. .err...I'm not sure I'm anything special, but I can do a mean Kickflip," Stevie said, warming slightly to Mr Barron. After all, anyone who liked skateboarding couldn't be all that bad.

But he had trusted too soon because the next thing Mr Barron said turned his world upside-down.

"I'm very pleased to hear that because I know you will enjoy Smithson as much as I do," he said.

Mr Barron looked firstly at his mother and then at his father with a beaming smile covering his bullet-shaped face. "You are all coming to live in Smithson, beginning next school term and my town will not only have two very talented and much needed veterinarians, but also a talented baseballer," he said winking at Jem who winked back, "and another Vegas with very special talents."

Before Stevie could get a word out in protest, Mr Barron turned directly to him and lowered his voice, speaking so that his family could not hear and making no mistake the comment was directed at Stevie.

"A skater with a mind full of talents for the extra-ordinary, much like myself and my son Jacob."

CHAPTER 4 - A NOT SO PLEASANT INTRODUCTION

The grey, overcast sky reflected Stevie's thoughts as the Vegas family drove into Smithson - a town of about 6000 inhabitants in what Stevie thought ruefully was the middle of nowhere. His old home of Valley Dale was only 20 minutes from the coast; more like a seaside village and had very little of the conservative veneer that seemed to typify inland towns like Smithson.

Stevie noticed the landscape changed the further inland they drove. Rolling green hills gave way to a flat landscape with fenced treeless paddocks that went on forever. The dry, hot summer had parched the land so that the paddocks were either brown or, at best, contained a corn or wheat crop ready for a harvest.

The whole family became more and more subdued as the trip wore on, as though they shared each other's thoughts that leaving Valley Dale might not have been such a good idea after all. Only their mother tried to lift everyone's mood with a forced cheeriness they knew she didn't feel.

"Come on you lot," she admonished. "Smithson will be fun. Jem you know all about their cricket facilities and Stevie, the town has the region's foremost skate facility in "Skateopia".

Stevie pushed the hair away from his eyes and gave his mum a look that said: "you tried and you failed."

Jem rolled his brown eyes. "Come on Mum," he said. "Smithson really sucks!" Before Mrs Vegas could disagree, Stevie pointed to the sign that said: "Welcome to Smithson - a town where dreams come true."

"I wonder whether it's actually nightmares that come true," Stevie murmured to himself. He could not shake the sense of unease that seemed to increase the closer they came to Smithson. A thought kept pushing its way to the surface, 'beware of friendly strangers'. He didn't know why he would have thought this and it seemed to have come from nowhere. It was also a somewhat alien thought for Stevie because, on the whole, he was a friendly and trusting boy and took people at face value - until he learned otherwise.

They passed through the main shopping centre and rounded a bend in the road. Stevie noticed they were on the outskirts of the town. The car began to climb a slight hill, out of which an enormous dark house seemed to rise. Stevie noticed for the first time that the brown farming paddocks had given way to a forest which was becoming thicker as they drove.

"Nearly there," Mr Vegas said, injecting the enthusiasm into his voice that he hoped would lift his family's spirits. He was a tall man, thin, but wiry and strong. He had grown up on his parent's farm at the foot of the mountains, tending to the farm's animals and had shown a knack for it before he moved to the city to study veterinary science. There he had met Stevie's mum Sylvia, a beautiful dark haired Canadian who beat her peers in just about every subject except the equine class. Smaller animals were really her thing and she had built their joint vet practice on the strength of her skills with dogs and cats while he had specialised in caring for the larger animals. They were a good team and he had generally followed her lead in most things, trusting her judgement, but relocating to Smithson had been his idea. Smithson was essentially a farming community and for Mr Vegas it was like going back home. This had been the deciding factor when he accepted Mr Barron's proposition. But as they journeyed further and further away from Valley Dale to a strange place which was so unlike their peaceful seaside village, Mr Vegas began to doubt the merit of the move. He pushed this thought away, concentrating instead on mustering the required enthusiasm and confidence which he did not really feel.

"Ok Vegas family," he said, maneuvering the Ford Territory deftly through the narrow gate. A dirt driveway led to a large bungalow surrounded by thick forest. "This is your new home!"

Jem was the first to speak. "Dad it's about two kilometres to town. And look at this forest. Gosh I'd hate to be walking home at night on my own."

Jem looked nervously across at his older brother as he always did when he felt nervous. He was waiting for Stevie to say something to make him feel better but Stevie had his mind on other things.

"Dad, who owns that house up on the top of the hill?" He pointed up the road to the sprawling mansion, half hidden by a thicket of large trees and an equally tall brick wall which enclosed the house from a prying public, he thought. It was less than a kilometre away from the Vegas' bungalow.

"Ah that house, or castle I should say, belongs to the Barron family," Mr Vegas answered.

"A bit close for comfort don't you think?" Stevie said.

Mr Vegas looked at his son, momentarily puzzled. "What do you mean Stevie? Chris Barron is one of the friendliest strangers I have ever met. It was quite a generous offer your mother and I received to come here. It will mean that you and Jem can now go to college...have the things we always wanted to give you."

His mother joined in. "Stevie...really...don't be like this. You'll settle in quickly, you'll see. How about a scout round town after lunch? I'm sure we can fit in a visit to Skateopia.

Stevie's face brightened. If there was one thing that eased the heavy feeling that seemed to hang over him since they turned off the highway to Smithson, it was the thought of skating. He really did need to practice. He reached for his skateboard; an EarthWind his mother had given him only last Christmas. It was a striking board with its red grip tape over a deck emblazoned with a black and gold eagle. When Stevie skated he felt like that eagle - at one with the air.

23

After lunch and an afternoon of unpacking, the Vegas family felt collectively better. They were all in high spirits as they approached the Smithson skate park.

"Right boys," Mr Vegas said. "You've got about an hour. Your mum and I'll finish the grocery shopping."

Jem and Stevie grabbed their boards. Stevie nodded to his father. "Right dad, we'll be here," and then turning to his mother, "...yes mum I'll keep an eye on Jem."

"I don't need looking after," Jem protested. Mrs Vegas smiled at her youngest child. "Ok then, you don't need looking after."

"Well, sometimes...maybe," he grinned. "And mum, don't forget the cookies and cream ice cream for tonight."

Alexander and Sylvia Vegas smiled at each other as they drove off, both harboring the same idea of filling the new fridge and pantry with treats for the boys in an effort to soften the alien feelings a new town was bringing.

Stevie watched the black Ford Territory disappear down the main street of Smithson and then turned his attention to Skateopia. The first thing that struck him was that it was huge. Street ramps had been positioned so boarders could ride from right to left without the slightest chance of collision. Connecting ramps meant that users could transfer tricks from one ramp to another and the Grind rails were just, well...simply awesome, he thought.

Stevie had never seen anything so sophisticated, not to mention that every radius of the park's curves, bends and quarter pipes were accurate down to the finest detail. This park had been built with the best design and materials money could buy and would be a pleasure to skate on. The rapture on his face must have been evident because he didn't feel the urgent tug on his T-shirt at first.

"Stevie, Stevie, come on." Jem's tone was urgent. "What? What!" Stevie answered in reply.

"Those guys over there...they don't look so friendly," Jem said, pointing to a group of about five boys who were

24

around Stevie's age. One boy was about to drop in at the six foot ramp, but before he did he called to Stevie.

"Hey you, new boy, show us what you got," he said.

Stevie looked directly at the boy. He was used to bullies and they didn't scare him. He noticed the boy's appearance though, not your typical skateboarder. This boy was well dressed to say the least - not the usual T-shirt and ripped jeans look, but rather he was dressed in black leathers. On the back of his jacket was a white skull logo Stevie had not seen before. It caught his attention.

"Who wants to know?" he answered back, catching a glimpse of the boy's face. Blonde hair framed a pointed face and almost black eyes, eyes that reminded him of someone but he couldn't think who.

The boy smiled as if to challenge Stevie. "Me, that's who, and I own Skateopia. Let's say if there was a king of Skateopia, it d be me."

Stevie felt a flicker of caution. He tried to read the boy's thoughts but felt a brick wall instead. This boy with the dark smile and flashing black eyes was somehow different. "Ok," he said joining the boy on the top of the ramp. "If that's how you want it. Nice intro though...not!"

Stevie stared down the ramp, gritted his teeth and pushed off hard. He felt his board move with him as he sailed downwards - down to the bottom of the ramp and then up the incline, gathering speed for the Pop Shove It spin he was about to do. Stevie felt the familiar thrill - ramp, air and sky. Rider and board were part of the same thing, and pure adrenalin combined with willpower and passion to be the best boarder ever. His momentum was enough to pull off a traditionally difficult triple Kickflip instead. The gathering crowd let out an applause that took Stevie by surprise. He was grinning with delight when he landed back on top of the ramp's platform only to be confronted with the stranger's menacing stare.

25

"Think you're good, do you?" the strange boy said. "Well I'll show you who's best and it's not you." With that the boy pushed off with lightening speed. Stevie's heart was in his mouth as he witnessed the boy execute a perfect Fingerflip Cannonball - one of the most difficult moves a skater can make. Landing back on the platform, the boy's look was one of triumph.

"For the record, my name's Barron.....Jacob Barron," he said without offering Stevie his hand. "And you...well...you're just lame to say the least. I've seen better Kickflips by a six year old."

"Like that is it?" Stevie said, pushing off again and anger darkening his usual friendly features. He was more determined than ever to outskate his opponent. As he pushed off for the second time, his mind was awhirl - the air around him electric as he performed the longest Airwalk he'd ever done, followed by a double Kickflip.

"Beat that," he almost shouted as he landed perfectly on the platform.

Jacob Barron's smile had long since faded from his face by the time Stevie had finished his stunt. Instead his mouth had formed into an angry thin line.

"You dare to challenge me?" he said. "We'll see about that! Let's go together and let the crowd judge eh? On my count...one...two...three..."

Without thinking, Stevie pushed off for a third time at precisely the moment Jacob exploded down the ramp. They were neck and neck as they came hurtling up the incline, both performing a triple Kickflip at the same time. Stevie could see Jacob's eyes flash with competitiveness as they sailed back down the ramp. The small crowd was cheering with excitement to see the two very evenly matched skaters dual for top position.

As Stevie was preparing to execute a Pop Shove It, he felt Jacob's mind closing in on his and, for a brief moment, his mind filled completely with the thought: "You're going to fall." It was enough to throw him off balance and he let go of his board, tumbling headlong down the ramp and coming to a stop at the bottom. The crowd let out a gasp and he thought he heard Jem call out to him. "Stevie, Stevie, Stevie!

With anger coursing through every fibre of his body he jumped to his feet, fist clenched and yelling at the top of his voice.

"You scumbag! He yelled at Jacob Barron. "You did this; you made me fall."

Barron threw back his head and laughed loudly, skating down to face him at the bottom of the ramp. "You're the rotten pig and a loser too," he said before kicking his board up and catching it deftly in his left hand. "I told you new boy, I'm the king of Skateopia...and don't you forget it. Next time you come here you better be prepared to skate for your life."

"Is that a threat?" Stevie said through clenched teeth. He concentrated hard and projected his thoughts. "I know what you've done and you better watch out."

For one very brief moment surprise crossed Barron's face. He stared at Stevie, angry and surprised at the same time.

"It's you who had better watch out!"

Jem skated down to Stevie, worry on his young face. "Stevie, mum and dad are here. We've got to go."

Stevie kicked up his board, catching it and turning his back on Barron.

"Come on Jem, let's get out of here. This place is full of cheats."

His parents were waiting for them at the car, eager for Stevie's pronouncement of the skate park's superior design. Instead, Stevie got sullenly into the car and stayed silent.

"Well young man?" Mr Vegas asked.

"I'd like to go back to the bungalow now dad."

Stevie's parents looked across at each other, knowing better than to continue questioning Stevie when he was angry. They assumed he had messed up a trick and would soon regain his usual good humor.

"Ok," Mr Vegas said, nodding knowingly to Jem. "We can talk about the skate park later. In the meantime I have excellent news for you both. Tonight we are visiting our newest friend, Chris Barron...and his son Jacob will also be there. He's about your age Stevie and Jem. Chris has kindly asked us to join him for dinner at the Barron estate."

Stevie couldn't believe what he'd heard. Surely his father wasn't serious. This would mean he would be the guest of the two people he dreaded the most in this new and strange place and the thought of being in the same room as them left him cold.

He shivered even though it was the middle of summer, looking out at the thickening forest as the sun was setting behind the hill, silhouetting the Barron estate so that it looked even more menacing at dusk than in the daylight.

"Great," he said to his father. "Can't wait."

CHAPTER 5 - NIGHT FALL AT THE BARRON ESTATE

Night was falling over Smithson as the Vegas family drove up the hill toward the Barron mansion. Everywhere the unfamiliar landscape caste its eerie shadow and their new home took on a dark and sinister appearance - more like a prop in a scary movie than a sleepy, mid western farming community.

The large stone entrance to the Barron estate with its overpowering wrought iron gates only added to the strangeness of the night, Stevie thought, capping off an equally strange day in the life of the Vegas family. Neither Stevie nor Jem wanted to accompany their parents to the Barron's and Stevie well remembered the dark, menacing black aura that had surrounded Mr Barron that night in Valley Dale. Very slowly the gates swung open as if to say whatever comes in may never get out. Stevie felt a chill go up his spine and shivered, despite the warmth of the family car.

Leaning over, Jem whispered: "This place is creepy."

"I agree," Stevie said in a whisper, so that his parents could not hear.

As the Vegas car pulled into the driveway, he could not help but notice the sheer size and overwhelming presence of the mansion. It contained no less than three wings and the main part of the house rose up four storey's into the night sky. Towers at the end of each wing gave it a gothic look and because of the darkness of the night, Stevie could not tell what material the home had been built from. He only saw the darkness of the stone and was not surprised in the slightest - only such a home could belong to Chris and Jacob Barron.

As the car came to a halt at the massive front entrance, Stevie felt momentarily dizzy. Thoughts popped into his head, unbidden and unwelcome. He could 'hear' Mr Barron talking to his son.

Mr Barron was telling his son to behave himself and watch his manners in front of their guests - after all the Vegas family were important...Stevie was important. Stevie sensed Jacob's dislike of his father's instructions...and there was the secret that could never be revealed...

"Stevie, Stevie, we're here darling. Are you getting out of the car?" His mother's far off voice penetrated his thoughts. As if coming out of a daze, Stevie shook his head to clear his thoughts. "...Err, yeah...sure mum."

He glanced over at his mum and thought he caught a look of apprehension on her face, but it was gone within an instant and Stevie thought he had imagined it. Was his mum as unsettled by the Barrons as he was? He was about to ask her if she was alright when the tall, oak and iron doors swung open for the Vegas family. Mr Barron stood welcoming them, a large smile on his face which never quite reached his eyes, Stevie thought. Instead his face remained fixed and unreadable; except for a glint of something in his eyes that Stevie realised was power. Here at the estate, Mr Barron's status was unquestionable. He was the master of his house and indeed of the town of Smithson which stretched out below them.

"Welcome, welcome." Mr Barron greeted the Vegas family enthusiastically. He smiled at Stevie. "And I hear you have already met a member of my family today Stevie. Aye? I hope that my son Jacob was a polite host to our newest citizens?"

"Yes sir," Stevie lied.

"And Skateopia? Was it up to your standards?"

"Yes sir," Stevie answered, not wanting to reveal anything to Mr Barron. He did not know whether Jacob had told his father about the encounter but he was determined not

30

to discuss it like this, in front of his parents and at Chris
Barron's front door.

Mr Barron gave him a rather odd look before resuming
his welcome, ushering the family into the drawing room.
Books lined every wall and the expansive room was
furnished with the best furniture money could buy. Sitting at
the end of the room, in front of a large fireplace was Jacob
Barron. Straight away Stevie felt a darkness descend upon
him, like someone was dimming the lights - the very same
feeling he had had in Valley Dale when he first met Chris
Barron. Surrounding Jacob was the same dark vapor, swirling
and pulsating, that had swarmed around Chris Barron. He
hadn't noticed it at the skate park, in the daylight, but here in
the mansion it was unmistakable.

Stevie drew in his breathe sharply. This house, these
people screamed danger at him. He looked furtively around
for the nearest doorway as if to plan an escape from the dark
forces he could sense were within the room. The thought
came to him that they were something other than human, but
he dismissed it as fanciful. Perhaps he was, after all, seeing
things that weren't there?

He glanced firstly at his mum, then his dad and then at
Jem. They were smiling warmly at Mr Barron and his son,
hopelessly oblivious to the black, swirling vapor that
crowned the Barrons. It took all Stevie's willpower to fight
down the urge to flee the room, much less greet Jacob Barron
as though nothing had happened that afternoon.

"Hello Stevie. Pleased to see you survived your fall."
Jacob smiled sweetly despite the challenge in his voice.

"Fall, what fall?" Mrs Vegas said, looking at Stevie her
face full of concern.

"It was nothing mum, really. My timing was out, that's
all. Nothing hurts. It's ok," he said reassuringly holding up
his arms which appeared absolutely normal and unscathed.

His mum smiled at him, shaking her head in mock
indignation. The worried expression on her face soon

changed to one of polite friendliness as she turned her attention back to the conversation Mr Vegas was now having with Mr Barron.

Stevie noticed he and Jacob were standing alone and he moved closer, lowering his voice. "Look, I don't know what you were playing at today, but you better watch yourself. I don't like playing games, much less with strangers you know would be a mistake to meet up with again."

"I think it's you who had better watch out Vegas," Jacob retaliated. "And I'd rather you weren't here tonight, but my father has other plans for your family."

Stevie grabbed Jacob roughly by the arm and led him to a quiet corner of the room, anxious that his parents did not overhear his conversation. His blue eyes were unwavering as he glared at the boy who had threatened him that afternoon. "What do you mean...plans for my family? What plans?"

A small grin formed at the corners of Jacob's mouth and he did not take his eyes off Stevie for a second. "You'll find out soon enough Vegas."

Stevie was about to 'search' Jacob's thoughts but the dinner bell rang and Mr Barron ushered his guests into the nearby dining room, putting an end to the boys' conversation.

"We'll continue this later Jacob," Stevie whispered as he rejoined his parents who were moving off towards the dining room with their host.

The dinner was typically rich and obviously expensive, consisting of salmon to start, followed by lamb from one of the nearby farms, and a tangy lemon dessert to finish. Stevie hardly touched his plate, preferring to talk to Jem rather than engage in conversation with Jacob Barron. Every now and then Mr Barron glanced in his direction and Stevie felt the pull of his thoughts. He had never felt like this before and it unnerved him, so he instinctively switched his thoughts to admiring the decor of the room - something neutral that would not betray his unease and even dislike of his hosts.

He was eager to leave the room once dessert had finished. "Umm...excuse me Mr Barron, but I need to use the toilet."

"Of course Stevie, straight through the drawing room and to your left. Would you like Jacob to accompany you?"

Stevie shook his head. "No. I mean no thank you," he said, meeting Chris Barron's suspicious gaze. "I won't be a minute," he said, turning to his parents and ignoring Jacob Barron's stare.

Once he was out of the room, Stevie let out a huge sigh of relief. It had almost been unbearable sitting at the table with a man he sensed was pure evil and his son who had thought nothing of causing Stevie to fall during a high speed stunt at the skate park. For the second time that night, he wondered just who the Barrons were but he had no answers, only questions.

He glanced around at his surroundings - he had re-entered the drawing room with its shelves stacked to the ceiling with books. Books, particularly old books, had always fascinated him and the Barron library had caught his attention earlier in the evening. He lingered in the room, looking closer at the selection on the nearby wall and eager to find out what subjects the Barron's enjoyed reading about - after all they were the strangest people Stevie had ever met. He wouldn't have been surprised to find a book about demons in their collection, given the dark aura surrounding Chris Barron.

Stevie smiled to himself. Demons, as if there were such a thing. That was the stuff television series and creepy movies were made of. He ran his fingers over the books, searching for a title that interested him. "The History of Smithson - from Indian Massacres to Modern Civilisation"; "18th Century Paganism"; "Prophesies of Peru"....

The Barron's literary taste was a little weird to say the least Stevie thought, as his finger moved across the titles of the books along the shelf. He was just about to give up his curious exploration when a small but thick book caught his attention. Its title was peculiar "Illuminators and Shadowcasters - Light and Dark Forces". Stevie reached for it without really knowing why, only that a feeling deep in his gut told him to take the book. He glanced around nervously, hoping he would not be discovered, and pushed the book into the large pocket of his hooded jumper. Putting his hands into his jumper pockets to try and disguise the telltale bulge, he walked calmly back to the dining room.

They were finishing dinner when he re-entered the room. Mr Barron was mesmerising his audience as usual and Jacob was staring sullenly into the fire. Stevie sat down quietly hoping no-one would notice the book he had just taken from the Barron's library.

"You found your way Stevie I gather." Mr Barron said, giving Stevie his full attention. Stevie was sure he could sense the guilt that was starting to grow within him. What on earth had possessed him to take the book?

"Err...yeah...no problems." Stevie said, glancing pointedly at his father and willing him to say that it was time they went home.

As if on cue Mr Vegas announced that while dinner was finer than some meals he had eaten in a restaurant, it was time to take a tired Vegas family home. Stevie could not have been more relieved at that moment. Thrusting his hands back into his pockets to conceal the book, he followed his dad out to the car. Without really knowing why, he quietened his mind, subduing the guilt he felt at stealing the book, and thought about skating - anything but the strange book he could feel beneath his fingers.

As the Vegas family were busy bundling themselves into the car, Mr Barron spoke directly to Stevie in a low voice. "You really are committed to your skating Stevie," he said.

Looking at him in the half light of the full moon, Stevie noticed the dark shroud that shadowed him and felt a tingle start in his spine. He looked at Mr Barron strangely - how had he known he was thinking about skating? And if he knew this, had he also known about the book? He couldn't be sure.

He got quickly into the car, mustering a courage he didn't feel and spoke directly to Mr Barron so that his parents could hear. "Thank you Mr Barron for dinner. Yes I enjoy skating and it is all I think about sometimes."

Chris Barron smiled back at Stevie. "You are very lucky Alexander and Sylvia to have such a talented son. I hope that now you are relocated to Smithson, and just a minute down the drive, that you will let me get to know your son better...As you know I enjoy fostering talent."

Mr and Mrs Vegas nodded enthusiastically. "Of course Mr Barron...Chris. Stevie and Jem could visit and Jacob is welcome to visit our boys any time."

Stevie grimaced in the dark light of the car. Didn't his parents see the obvious - that visiting the Barron estate was the last thing he wanted to do. His fingers closed around the book in his pocket and a strange thrill went through his body. He couldn't wait to get to the bungalow to start reading.

CHAPTER 6 - SHADOWCASTERS AND ILLUMINATORS

Stevie glanced at the clock beside his bed: 10.30pm. He yawned and snuggled even deeper into the feathery doona and picked up the strange book from his bedside table. It was old, very old and bound in thick black leather. A twinge of guilt ran through him for stealing it from the Barron estate, but he pushed it aside. The Barrons, after all, were at the very least strange, though Stevie suspected they were a little more than strange. Evil perhaps? He was sure the book held a clue as to who they were and why they were so fascinated with him, and he was determined to get to the bottom of it even if it meant staying up past midnight.

He propped his pillows up so he could half sit in bed and got ready for a long night. Illuminators, what on earth were they, he thought, and Shadowcasters - it sounded like something out of a bad fairytale and definitely not real. The night outside his window seemed to grow even darker as he picked up the heavy black book. Far off an owl hooted into the night. Stevie sank even further into the warm doona thankful he was indoors and began to skim through the pages, stopping at the chapter which described Illuminators.

"Illuminators can be found in any ordinary community, but they are far from ordinary.

They always display Extra Sensory Perception (ESP) which is highly developed from a young age. This ability to read thoughts often creates an affinity or bond with animals. In addition to their ESP, Illuminators can, when their powers have developed sufficiently, make events happen through their thoughts.

"Illuminators bring light where there is darkness and serve the forces for good. They sense the darkness within others and are able to see the aural light or shadow that

surrounds every human being. They bear the mark of a light bringer - a small star on their right shoulder...."

Stevie sat bolt upright. The mark they were referring to had been visible on his right shoulder ever since he could remember - a small star-shaped birthmark his parents used to say ran in the Vegas family. He hadn't thought anything of it, assuming it was just a normal mark and that everybody had some distinguishing spot or freckle or birthmark that made them unique. He had even felt quite proud that he carried the Vegas mark. He ran his hands over it and shook his head. Surely....it couldn't be?

But the more he read of the strange book, the more he knew that what he read was the truth behind the mystery, both his own unexplained gifts and possibly the black auras that surrounded the Barrons. It was beginning to make sense - all the strange thoughts that invaded his head when he was around others, knowing what they were going to say before they said it. And the times when he knew which angle to take to execute a perfect McTwist. His reflexes had always been razor sharp hadn't they? And simple things too, like telling his mum which lane to take in the supermarket car park so she could get a park...He was always 100% right, every time.

The more he thought about it, the more it made sense - even the part about seeing the light or shadow around people. Hadn't he seen the dark shroud surrounding Mr Barron? Hadn't he always seen the bright, shimmering light which surrounded his Aunt Bessie?

The clock beside his bed ticked over to midnight and the night closed in. Stevie read on, stopping at the section on Shadowcasters.

"Shadowcasters are the seekers of power and riches and they know greed, manipulation and hate well in others because it lives within them too. They covet what they don't have and they seek to possess everyone and everything in their path. They serve the forces of darkness and are capable of great destruction with the assistance of those they serve from the other worlds. They rise to positions of power within society and often hold high office. They are great studiers of history, for they increase their knowledge of the present by learning of the mistakes of the past, careful not to repeat them. They study human weakness and are able to grant what others seek. However in accepting gifts and rewards from the Shadowcasters, beware - they extract a high price for their favor..."

Stevie could read no further. What did this mean? He stared hard out of the window, hearing the eerie hoot of the far off owl again. The wind had picked up, catching at the enormous pine trees which surrounded the house. It whipped through their stately branches as though it commanded the power of the earth itself. He blinked against the gathering darkness outside his window and thought hard.

Was he an Illuminator? He could no longer deny the truth to himself. It hit him like a punch and he shook his head from side to side, exhaling the air that seemed to be building in his lungs. He carried the mark and he could read minds; sense things about people that he had no way of knowing. In the last 12 months he had felt a power growing within him - at times he even thought he had made something happen - like the time in the school gym when Jem was being bullied. The knowledge that he was no ordinary 12 year old overwhelmed him in that moment. The clock ticked over to 1pm but he was only aware of the night passing.

If he was an Illuminator, then what did that make the Barrons - Shadowcasters? Stevie thought back to the first time he had met Chris Barron and to the dark aura that surrounded him, seemingly spiraling out from him in black shards. He thought about the atmosphere that had accompanied his visit to Valley Dale - one of encroaching evil that seemed to arise from the depths of somewhere Stevie could not name. He had known even then that Chris Barron was a dangerous man and the first meeting with his son Jacob confirmed the son was no different from the father. They were one of a kind, and most likely Shadowcasters.

What did they want with him? Worse still, his family? He had to talk this over with someone before he exploded. It felt like he was carrying a huge burden, too great a load for a boy whose sole focus up to that point had been skating. He thought hard. And then he remembered.

Aunt Bessie. AUNT BESSIE! That's it. He had seen the shimmering white aura surrounding her. She always knew what he was going to say before he finished his sentence. She had been coming and going, visiting the Vegas household, since they were babies. He was particularly close to Aunt Bessie because he always felt she understood him the best in his family. He suddenly smiled; a huge smile of relief as a plan began to form in his mind. First thing in the morning he would ring her and ask her to come and stay. She would know what to do. She had to know. If she didn't...Stevie didn't even want to entertain the thought. First things first he thought, reaching over to turn off the light. Sleep was starting to spread its warm, comforting blanket over him as the images of Aunt Bessie played in his mind. She was smiling, and it put him at ease, enough to drift off to sleep finally.

All will be well.....that was the last thought he had before the shriek of the alarm clock woke him, far too early considering his late night.

CHAPTER 7 - ANOTHER DAY, ANOTHER BULLY

He raced downstairs, aware he was late and his mum would not be happy with him. They had planned to be at his new school early, to meet the principal and teachers and tour the school and its facilities. Smithson Elementary was supposed to be one of the better regional public schools with a reputation for turning out excellent sportspeople and, of all things, historians.

Stevie smiled when he learnt of the school's achievements - he could keep up with the best at a skate park but he had never managed more than a pass in history. Maths was definitely his best subject. He particularly liked its formulas and the problem solving, often applying these skills when he had to estimate his line and length before a difficult jump at the skate park. History, he felt, was best left to old people and, anyway, he would much prefer to concentrate on the future as something new and exciting and full of hope and optimism, not wars and battles and sieges. As he ran downstairs, he remembered that Shadowcasters were students of history. This thought immediately prompted his resolve to call Aunt Bessie.

"Stevie...Stevie..." He heard his mum's frantic calls and quickened his pace, half sliding down the last section of the banister. When he got to the kitchen Jem was tucking into pancakes smeared with his favorite topping - butter of all things. His dad was dressed in a suit he noticed, to go to work at Smithson Veterinary and his mum was stirring a steaming hot pot of porridge which was his favorite breakfast.

"There's local honey on the table," she said without turning to note his arrival at the breakfast table, "and I've cut up fresh bananas for you too."

Stevie marveled at her organisation and wished he had inherited some of it. "Thanks mum, just what I felt like." He brushed his fringe away from his blue eyes and gave her a sweet smile. He loved his mum...and his dad and his brother, and seeing them all sitting around the breakfast table reminded him of the urgency of getting in touch with Aunt Bessie. He was just about to suggest his aunt visit when his mum interrupted his thoughts.

"Stevie...are you listening to me? Really all you seem to be able to focus on these days is skating..."

"Uh...Oh yeah, mum, what were you saying?" Stevie asked.

"I was just saying to your father that Aunt Bessie called this morning and will be coming to visit for a couple of weeks this Friday."

"What?" Stevie said. "But I was just thinking about her last night."

His mother did not look the least surprised. "So? What Stevie? You know that sort of coincidence is not unusual in this family."

Stevie looked sideways at Jem and noticed the big grin on his face. "Yeah." Jem replied. "It's no biggie - stuff like that is always happening to us."

His father put down the newspaper he was half reading during all the chatter at the breakfast table. "Well Vegas family, I'm off to work - first day; I want to be early." He leant over and kissed his wife on the cheek. "Will you be alright with the boys?"

"No problems," she said. "And speaking of early starts, it's time to hit the road Stevie and Jem. Smithson High awaits."

The gates of Smithson High swung open to allow the Vegas' Ford Territory entry and to reveal a large, old brick building that reminded Stevie more of a prison than school. Nothing surprised him about Smithson and everything he was seeing only confirmed the strangeness of the place, like it

41

was somehow encircled by an invisible wall of darkness that Stevie couldn't explain. He just knew that he had expected the worst to happen as soon as he drove through the town's entrance and so far it had.

Principal Hawker was thorough in his introduction to life at Smithson High. Before first period had begun, Stevie and Jem knew all about the rules and regulations that governed life at the school and about the school's biggest donator to the school Board: Chris Barron. While the connection between Principal Hawker and Chris Barron did not surprise Stevie, the dark shroud which hovered around the Principal did. Stevie kept his distance and promised in front of his mum to faithfully abide by the school's rules.

Stevie glanced sideways at Jem's stony face. He knew that Jem hated rules - not that he was unco-operative; on the contrary, Jem was one of the best behaved students at Valley Dale High. But Valley Dale also didn't require a military-like obedience to authority either. Stevie knew the road ahead at Smithson High would be rough for his younger brother. He put his hand reassuringly on Jem's shoulder and whispered: "It's alright mate, we'll get used it - since when have rules every bothered us?"

"What was that?" Principal Hawker said, turning to face Stevie.

"Oh...nothing sir...I was just telling my brother that we'll get used to Smithson High, in time."

"I hope that it will not take you too long to settle in here Stevie and Jem. We find, here at Smithson High, that the sooner you accept your new surroundings, and the rules we have here, the more...comfortable school life will be," Principal Hawker said.

Stevie was not absolutely sure, but he wondered if the principal had been reading his thoughts. Smithson, and its high school, were beginning to feel increasingly strange. Actually a little more than strange. They were beginning to feel threatening. Attempting to hide his thoughts, Stevie replied that he and Jem would be fine. "We're used to rules," he said, speaking to Principal Hawker directly.

He then turned to his mum and after assuring her they'd be ok, Stevie and Jem waved her off and were directed to their classrooms. He winked at Jem as they veered off in two separate directions.

"I'll catch you at recess Jem," he said, noticing Jem's sullen expression.

Stevie made his way quickly down the corridor and to the classroom Mr Hawker had assigned to him. He slowly opened the door to a roomful of crowded 12 year olds, all eager to check out the new kid. The teacher greeted him warmly, something Stevie welcomed after the coldness of Principal Hawker. Introducing him to the class, she directed him to an empty seat near a young Korean boy. He smiled as Stevie sat down and Stevie made a mental note that two people, so far, had been welcoming that day.

However the warmth of the greetings was soon replaced by the realisation Stevie was to share a classroom with Jacob Barron, who was sitting two rows away with a tall, blonde haired boy. Their eyes locked together in mutual dislike and, for an instant, Stevie thought he saw hatred in Jacob's face.

"I'll see you at recess," Jacob mouthed silently, pointing his finger at Stevie.

Stevie shrugged him off, turning away and shifting his attention to his desk companion. He put out his hand. "Stevie Vegas," he said.

"Hi, I'm Tom Lee," he replied.

"Pleased to meet you Tom," Stevie said, shaking his hand warmly.

"I've seen you before," Tom whispered. "At the skate park...you're good, but no match for Jacob Barron."

Stevie looked puzzled. "Of course I'm a match for Barron," he said, lowering his voice so the teacher who was busy writing on the blackboard couldn't hear.

"You're not you know," Tom said, looking at him intently, "'cause Jacob Barron is the dirtiest competitor there is. You don't stand a chance against him. I know, because he cost me my skating career."

Stevie looked at the stranger to see if he was joking with him. "What do you mean the dirtiest skater?"

Tom held up a misshapen wrist that looked like it had been badly broken in several places. "Fancy having one of these?" Tom said, trying to make light of his claw-like hand. Stevie's jaw dropped.

"It's not so bad," Tom shrugged, not wanting Stevie's pity. "But seriously, stay away from him. Nothing good will come of it. Stay away from Barron and the blonde haired guy sitting next to him. Barron and his mate McCauley will try and bring you down, whether it's on or off the skateboard."

Stevie started copying the history lesson from the board. "You don't need to worry about me," he told Tom. "I can look after myself." Tom looked doubtful.

"I mean it," Stevie said with a defiant toss of his fringe. "Barron, McCauley, whoever, they better watch out for me, 'cause I'm not scared of their kind - they're just bullies and the only way to treat bullies is to come at them twice as hard so they remember not to come back a second time."

Tom couldn't help himself, for the first time in months he relaxed. He liked this new boy and if he couldn't skate competitively anymore, then maybe he would teach him his own specially modified Kickflip. If this new kid could beat Jacob Barron, now that would be kind of like payback. He tucked his misshapen hand back under his desk and began writing down the history notes with his good hand, a smile playing, ever so slightly, at the corners of his mouth.

CHAPTER 8 - RAINBOW DREAMING

Stevie spent the rest of the day at Smithson High, reasonably uneventfully. When the final buzzer went for the afternoon, he found Jem amongst a sea of faces and hurried to the car park aware their mum would be eager for a 'first day' report.

"How did you two boys go?" his mum asked, slight worry lines creasing her normally smooth brow.

"Ok...I guess," Jem said, with just a hint of distraction in his voice. Stevie glanced over at his little brother who, like his mum, was normally calm and happy with his lot in life. Today, though, Stevie could sense that Jem was worried about something else he didn't know about. Immediately Jacob Barron and McCauley flashed through his mind.

"Jem were you ok at lunchtime - I couldn't get away from class until late and I missed you in the playground," Stevie asked.

"Yeah," Jem replied in a low voice so his mum wouldn't hear. "I was alright - if you call being beaten up by bullies ok."

"What? Why didn't you come get me...I'll deal with these scumbags. Don't worry Jem...they better watch out for themselves tomorrow..."

Jem's eyes flashed with anger. "No," he whispered, anger in his voice. "Leave off, Stevie. I can fight my own battles. You'll only make things worse."

Stevie stared hard at his brother. He didn't understand Jem's attitude. He was just about to dig deeper for the reason his younger brother didn't want his help when his mother interrupted them.

"Hey you two," Mrs Vegas said. "What's all the fighting about?"

It was Stevie's turn to sulk. "Nothing mum. It's nothing. Can you let me out here? I think there's a good track home. It follows the river and it's not far."

His mother was about to protest, after all this was still a strange place to the Vegas family, but she thought better of it. She sensed a little bit of flexibility was needed to smooth the way, given both her sons looked like they were about to explode.

"Ok Stevie. I know that track. Your father and I went for a walk last night - it's pleasant enough and I think quite safe."

She pulled the Territory over to let Stevie out at the clearing. The Vegas bungalow was just in sight up ahead in the distance and the walk by the river might calm him down.

Sylvia Vegas smiled brightly at her son. "Don't be too long darling. I've made a double chocolate chip mud cake for afternoon tea."

Not even the thought of his mum's rich chocolate cake brought a smile to his face. Between the Barrons, this strange town and now Jem's mysterious attitude, Stevie was in no mood to snap out of his bad temper. "I won't be long," he called to his mum as the car pulled away.

His eyes sought out the pathway down to the river. Smithson boasted a major river running through its borders, the Katonga River. Stevie knew the area around Smithson had a rich history, including being home to the Indians centuries ago.

He made his way down the rocky pathway to the river. Up ahead the track wound through the welcome shade of the pine trees just a few feet away from the water's edge. Here and there, along the river's banks, were tables and benches that had obviously been built to accommodate the many picnickers in summer. As it was Spring Stevie was the sole walker on the trail that day.

He couldn't help but go over the events of the last weeks in his head as he walked, playing and replaying key scenes in his mind, as if it would help him make sense of the riddles that had been a feature of his life since Chris Barron first appeared in his living room. He was deep in thought when something caught his eye. Up ahead in the near distance was what looked like an Indian camped by the river. As he drew closer, he saw the Indian was dressed in jeans and a flannelette shirt - quite an unremarkable costume, Stevie thought, for an Indian - however as he entered the campsite something caught his eye and literally mesmerised him to the spot. The Indian's long, straight, pitch black hair and his aura held him transfixed, as if he had seen a vision from another world. The man's aura was a swirling white mass of light with the colors of the rainbow shooting out from a piercing white centre. Stevie had never seen anything like the brilliance that circled the man. Despite himself, and the fact this was a complete stranger, Stevie walked up to the man unannounced and uninvited.

"Uh...hello...my name's Stevie Vegas," he said realising as he finished his sentence he was trespassing in this strange man's camp. He shifted awkwardly from one foot to another waiting for the man answer.

The man who was sitting on a log in front of a small camp fire, continued to stir the smoky substance cooking on the fire. "I know." The man didn't look up when spoke, and didn't address anyone in particular but more to the wind which had begun to rise and blow the leaves around on the ground.

"You know my name?" Stevie questioned. Immediately, a picture of a white, shimmering stone in the shape of a star flashed through his mind. In that instant he tried to read the man's thoughts but could see nothing in his mind's eye. He was conscious of the Indian's gaze now upon him, though he felt no hostility from the man. Rather, he felt a strange kinship and he knew instantly the man meant him no harm.

"There is no need for words Stevie Vegas is there?" The man was looking directly at Stevie now with his piercing

47

green, tawny-like eyes but no words came out of his mouth, rather he was talking through the power of thought.

"No," Stevie replied just as silently. "But, why...who are you?"

The Indian smiled gently. "My name is Chipara which is the word for rainbow in my tribe. I am here to help you and to remind you that something good always follows something bad, as long as you have faith in yourself and in the good that is always present in humanity."

Stevie smiled too, as an image of a rainbow filled his mind. He continued his thought conversation with the Indian. "How do you know something bad is happening - I sense it and fear it but I don't know what I can do about it? I am just a boy who can read people's thoughts."

The Indian patted the space next to him on the log, for Stevie to sit down by the fire. Stevie's gaze was immediately drawn to the flames.

"There is so much you do not understand yet Stevie Vegas but surely you know you are special, that you are an Illuminator - a bringer of light and hope to many. You must know that you are here in Smithson for a reason and that it is your destiny to face the Shadowcasters."

At the mention of Shadowcasters, Stevie began to feel the fear at the base of his spine. He was no match for the likes of Chris Barron and he felt his confidence give way to a sinking feeling that had now moved to the pit of his stomach.

The Indian touched his brow lightly and the fear began to subside. "Your fear of the unknown creates the anxiety you currently feel Stevie Vegas, yet there is nothing to fear but fear itself. You must know that you have talents you have not even realised yet."

Stevie shook his head in doubt and looked into the Indian's eyes. He had so many unanswered questions. He felt himself drawn into the dark pools of the stranger's eyes, into the blackness of them. At the end of a long, dark tunnel he saw a white shimmering light which glowed so brightly

Stevie immediately looked away. "That is your core power Stevie Vegas."

Chipara continued to project his thoughts into Stevie's mind. "It is the light that shines within you that illuminates the darkness. You have the power to read minds, but you also have a power to transform thought into actions and this is the power of creation. Your greatest trial will be to learn how to use this power wisely and when the time comes for the lesson you must learn, you will not fail."

Stevie began to protest, silently, against the Indian's words but Chipara continued.

"You are an Illuminator and there are others like you. When you need help, it will be there and remember help can be found in the strangest of places and when you least expect it."

Stevie began to move toward the light but he felt himself drawn away and back to reality. Realising he had closed his eyes at some point he opened them, slowly, squinting at the brightness of the sun overhead. He looked around hoping to see Chipara but the river bank was bare.

Had he been dreaming? As quickly as the doubt entered his mind he knew in his heart that Chipara had been real. Years of living with the unexpected meant Stevie had kept an open mind. He got to his feet and brushed the grass off his clothes. The Vegas bungalow was just up ahead. As he made his way up the river bank leading to his backyard he thought of Chipara's words that help can sometimes be found when you least expect it. So often he'd been struggling with a problem and an answer appeared, whether it was a new skateboarding mentor, or through a teacher. Sometimes even a friend would say the right thing at the right time. He knew Chipara was right - sometimes help did appear at the right time, when he needed it most.

He could smell the sweetness of the chocolate cake in the air from the Vegas bungalow, making a path to his nostrils and realised he was quite hungry. From the back of the house the sound of laughter greeted him and, as he walked down the hallway to the kitchen, he glimpsed a familiar face.

"Aunt Bessie!" he said. "I didn't think you were coming until Friday."

A huge grin transformed Aunt Bessie's normally stern features. "Well young man I had a feeling you could do with a visit."

CHAPTER 9 - AUNT BESSIE AND THE CURSED STONES

Aunt Bessie's twinkling eyes greeted Stevie as he entered the kitchen, along with his mother's warm smile. He stooped over and gave his Aunt a kiss and big hug hello and returned his mum's smile before reaching for a piece of the enormous chocolate upon chocolate cake in the centre of the kitchen table.

He sat down, taking in the happy domestic scene before him. Jem was busy munching away on a humungous slice of cake. He smiled to himself at the sight of Jem's chocolate encrusted mouth. At least he looked happy...better than the sullen, almost angry expression he wore at the end of the school day. Next he turned his attention to Aunt Bessie, trying to hide his thoughts about his encounter with Chipara. Aunt Bessie had an uncanny knack of picking up on other people's thoughts. Much like himself, he thought.

"Aunt Bessie it's great to see you again, and a surprise visit. I was only just thinking about you."

Aunt Bessie gave her nephew her full attention. "Well Stevie, I must have picked up on your thoughts because I felt it was about time I checked up on you and Jem now you've settled in Smithson, and make sure you are all well and happy."

Her glance fell momentarily on Jem and a worried look crossed her face, momentarily. She turned back to Stevie's mum with a bright smile though and continued her conversation about the night's dinner.

While she was chatting with Sylvia Vegas, Stevie had the opportunity to study his Aunt a bit more closely.

Aunt Bessie was as old as she was wise. He knew that for certain. She had a kindly but stern face and you knew instinctively she didn't suffer fools for long. Stevie also knew that she had a heart of gold underneath a tough exterior, particularly when it came to her family. She was his grandmother's sister, which made her his great aunt really. However his mum was an only child and Aunt Bessie had been visiting for as long as he could remember. She was 'close' family and Stevie loved that she understood him...and his special ways. She had never made a secret of the fact that she always 'knew' when a family member was in trouble and it came as no surprise to him she turned up, seemingly out of the blue. She always encouraged Stevie to talk openly about his impressions of the people he had met - particularly where he too had 'picked up' thoughts and feelings from them.

Stevie watched her as she explained her recipe for meatloaf and he guessed that would be on the menu for dinner. His tummy began to rumble, despite the big slice of chocolate cake he had just devoured, and he realised the walk had made him hungry. He began to think about what Chipara had told him, forgetting his Aunt's presence. His thoughts were interrupted by the feeling of Aunt Bessie's penetrating stare.

"Stevie, I was wondering if you could help me upstairs with my suitcases."

"Absolutely Aunt Bessie." He finished his cake and picked up the set of blue suitcases in the nearby hallway.

"Now give me one of those," Aunt Bessie said, reaching for the heaviest.

He began to protest.

"I'm fine," she insisted, ignoring his protests. He had to admit she appeared to have strength beyond her years. He knew that at 62 she was as fit as someone 10 years younger, thanks to her active lifestyle. One thing you wouldn't find Aunt Bessie doing was sitting in a chair in front of the TV for hours on end.

She was an active member of her seaside community and it seemed to Stevie that she was always helping everyone with their troubles. He remembered that once she even helped the police solve a missing person's case. Thanks to Aunt Bessie's help the runaway teenager was found at a roadhouse 50 kilometres from where she had hitched a ride out of the troubled home she inhabited. Aunt Bessie was a constant visitor at that teenager's house in the months that followed and the girl never tried running away again.

And then there was the time she saved a young toddler from an oncoming car. Stevie couldn't recall all the details as the near accident had happened when he was much younger, but he did remember his Aunt had grabbed the girl at the last minute averting what would have been sure death for the young toddler. The strange thing was the car driver said his Aunt seemed to come from nowhere to save the girl. He had also told the newspapers he felt compelled to brake suddenly, long before he saw the girl who had been playing on the road about 50 metres ahead. Most people didn't bother with the details, only the fact his Aunt had been there to save the girl....Mary Lou. Stevie even remembered her name because the story had made such an impression on him.

Before he had a chance to put the suitcase down in the guest room, his thoughts were interrupted by Aunt Bessie's urgent whisper. "Stevie, you must listen to me."

His Aunt put her suitcase down and sat down at the nearby window seat. "Quickly, we haven't time. Come sit beside me. I need to talk you about Chris Barron."

Stevie's face must have shown his surprise, but he said nothing, sitting quietly beside her, wondering what on earth was so urgent and why his Aunt had raised the subject of Chris Barron.

"You know Stevie that you and I are 'special', don't you?"

Stevie nodded, giving his Aunt his full attention.

"I didn't want to have this talk with you just yet...I wanted to wait a couple of years until you could take in what I'm about to tell you. But I sense danger around you and your family...have done ever since you moved to Smithson. I fear...well..." Her voice trailed off.

Stevie turned to her, intensity in his eyes that had not been there before. "It's alright Aunt Bessie; you don't need to tell me. I already know I am an Illuminator and I'm guessing you are too?"

She nodded, a look of relief spreading across her face. "Perhaps I underestimated you Stevie. I am picking up that you have learnt a great deal since Mr Barron arrived in your life. You sense the danger too." He nodded silently.

"I feel it's time you understood more about Illuminators and more about me. I can also tell you a great deal about Chris Barron as I have known of him for many years. You also need to know about one of the most powerful and negative objects on this earth...the cursed stones."

The cursed stones! Stevie had never heard of anything like this before and of all the strange things that had happened to him in the past month or so, this was the strangest. How can stones be powerful? He was about to ask this question when Aunt Bessie put her fingers to her lips as if to silence him.

"Ssshh, Stevie. We haven't much time. You will need to listen carefully."

For the second time that afternoon, Stevie fell under the spell of wise Elders and began to listen intently to Aunt Bessie's words.

Aunt Bessie leant closer, lowering her voice so that no-one else could share the secrets she was about to give her nephew.

"You know already about Illuminators and I'm guessing that you also know that every positive has a negative side."

Stevie looked slightly puzzled by the explanation, but Aunt Bessie continued.

"There are always two sides to the coin - everything has its opposite and so it is with Illuminators and Shadowcasters. Just as Illuminators bring light and do their best to interrupt evil, so the Shadowcasters spread not only evil but the temptation to do evil. Do you know what I mean by that Stevie?"

Stevie shook his head. "Not entirely Aunt Bessie".

Aunt Bessie continued. "Shadowcasters use their influence on those around them so that they follow them and are capable of just as much evil as they are...that way the darkness spreads. It is our job, the job of the Illuminators, to show others there is a better path. Have you ever noticed that with every Shadowcaster there appears another to do their bidding?"

Stevie understood. "Yes, now that you point it out, Jacob Barron has an offsider McCauley and he is just as bad as Barron. And I wouldn't be surprised if Principal Hawker was a follower of Chris Barron's."

"That's right," Aunt Bessie said. "There is power in numbers and the Shadowcasters know this. That is why they so actively try and recruit people Stevie."

Stevie nodded, thinking of gangs of bullies and mob rule. Even dictatorships didn't survive without support and fear and, eventually, dominance of all around.

"And that's why I'm here Stevie; to lend my support to the battle you are most surely fighting. You see, Chris Barron knows you are becoming more and more aware of your special abilities and that the world of the Illuminators is currently, as we speak, preparing to support you in the days ahead. In fact, you may have already been contacted if my sensing is correct?"

Stevie looked at her, surprise and confusion in his eyes. He had never seen this side of Aunt Bessie before. She was intense and her words carried an urgency he did not want to ignore.

"I met an Indian called Chipara, down by the river today," Stevie answered.

"Yes Stevie, I sensed his presence here because he too appeared to me when I was just a little older than you. I'm not sure who he is or how he gets here, or even if he is real, but I do know that it is of the utmost importance that you listen to the words he had for you. These words will come back to you...to help you when you most need them."

Stevie fell silent; trying to take in everything he had been told.

His Aunt Bessie continued. "Once the Shadowcasters know of an Illuminator, they do their best to recruit them to their side and to use the powers of Illumination for evil. That is why Chris Barron is trying so hard to please your parents, because he knows that this is the best way to get to you. Once he has seduced you and your family with material gifts such as money and, in your case, the best skating facilities and opportunities, it will be easy to convince you that he is someone you should listen to and follow."

"I will never do that," Stevie said through clenched teeth.

"There is something else," his Aunt whispered.

Stevie's eyes widened, as if what she had just told him wasn't enough.

"Shadowcasters draw most of their power from ancient stones that have been ingrained with spells caste by the first Shadowcasters centuries ago and handed down through the generations. These ancient stones - we Illuminators call them 'cursed' stones - allow the Shadowcasters to draw upon the wisdom of their Elders so that they can use this knowledge to increase their power. Most of us, even normal human beings, increase our knowledge and our power with age. The Shadowcasters take a short cut, if you like, through possessing the cursed stones and calling upon them when they need to perform unspeakable acts of evil. I am frightened Stevie, to be totally honest, that Barron will use his cursed stones to try and turn you away from the Illuminator's way."

For the second time that night, Stevie felt the anger explode within. "I told you before Aunt Bessie, I will never join with the Shadowcasters...no matter what."

Aunt Bessie gave him a gentle smile and patted his arm. "There Stevie, don't you worry. I know you would never do such a thing. You are stronger than that, but I am going to make doubly sure that no harm comes to you."

"How Aunt Bessie? How are you going to do that?" Stevie said.

The gentleness was now gone from Aunt Bessie's face and Stevie noticed she was deadly serious when she spoke. "We are going to steal Barron's cursed stone right from underneath him!"

If it wasn't so serious, Stevie would have burst out laughing, but something in his Aunt's expression stopped him. For the first time in his life, he could see the face of an Illuminator in Aunt Bessie - bravery, daring and a kindness that meant she was prepared to risk her safety for someone else and for what was right.

"I know you have a plan Aunt Bessie, because I can read it in your mind. I also know that you have arranged for Chris Barron to be called away suddenly to a meeting in Lake View, some 50 kilometres away from Smithson."

For the first time that night Aunt Bessie relaxed and let a huge smile spread from cheek to cheek, a bit mischievously actually, and now Stevie couldn't help but join her.

"You are getting quite good at this, aren't you Stevie Vegas," she said, gently tussling his hair. "Oh and by the way young man," she added, "bring your skateboard...we'll need it before the night's through."

"We are going to do this tonight?" Stevie said.

His Aunt nodded. "There is no better moment than the present," she said.

"But Aunt Bessie, you've just got here..."

"Nonsense," he Aunt replied, cutting him off mid sentence. "I've been with you since you got to Smithson Stevie, only you just never knew it. In fact, I've been watching over you all your life, knowing that one day you would come into your Illuminator powers. And that day is today."

Stevie's eyes widened, though he said nothing other than: "Tonight?"

His Aunt nodded, and Stevie felt her determination in the half light of the room. It was the determination of an Illuminator who didn't back down to anyone.

CHAPTER 10 - AN ACE UP HER SLEEVE

His Aunt Bessie changed before dinner into a simple black tracksuit - not the kind of attire appropriate for dinner given his parents had dressed up in honor of their first family meal with Aunt Bessie, but at 62 they all thought it better for her to be comfortable than formal. Only Stevie knew she had dressed appropriately for the night ahead.

After an excellent dinner of meatloaf and mixed spring vegetables and some more of his mum's delicious chocolate cake, his Aunt began to yawn at the dinner table.

"I don't know Sylvia," she said, turning to his mum. "You always knew how to cook a beautiful dinner but I am not as young as I used to be. I'm afraid a big meal at night always starts me yawning."

His mum was both pleased that Aunt Bessie had enjoyed her meal, but worried that the trip to Smithson had been long and tiring for her. His dad echoed his wife's concern.

"Well Aunt Bessie," he said. "Don't stand on ceremony, you know you can treat our house like your own and if you feel like going to bed, then go."

Stevie took his cue from his Aunt and began yawning widely too.

"What? Is this catching?" his mum said, laughing at the sight of Stevie and Aunt Bessie yawning in unison.

"No mum," Stevie answered. "But it has been a big day and you know...I'm not as young as I used to be."

The Vegas family let the tensions of their day go and laughed heartily at Stevie's joke. All except Jem.

"Jem is everything alright?" his Aunt enquired, worry replacing the merriment in her tone.

Jem's blue eyes clouded over for a second before he looked defiantly back at his Aunt.

"Why would anything be wrong?" he said. "We have a new house and my parents have new jobs, even if the house does belong to the Barrons and the jobs were provided by the Barrons and the school is run by the Barrons..."

"Jem!" his father protested. "The Barrons have been nothing but kind to us. You should remember to be grateful."

His Aunt interrupted them, determined to avoid the fight that was brewing between Jem and Mr Vegas. "Now Alexander, Jem is perhaps a little tired, like us all. Can I suggest that we leave our catching up on the family news until tomorrow, when we are in a better frame of mind? After all, you and Sylvia must surely be tired too."

Mr Vegas softened. Out of all his wife's relatives, Aunt Bessie was his favorite and she could twist him around her little finger. "Uh...yes...I suppose you are right. But Jem I want to talk to you about this tomorrow. Ok?"

Jem nodded silently, before excusing himself and making a quick getaway to his bedroom.

Stevie turned to his mum. "Do you need a hand with the dishes?"

"No darling, and that goes for you too Aunt Bessie, they are all going straight into the brand new dishwasher Mr Barron had installed in the bungalow only yesterday."

His dad smiled. "See, we really are lucky to have such a great friend. Chris thinks of everything."

Aunt Bessie nodded, if only a little cautiously. "Yes Alexander, but I will say this and I know it goes without saying, that the Vegas family was very happy in Valley Dale and Smithson will need to live up to that."

"Of course," his father replied. "It is only early days. If it turns out that even one of us is unhappy, we will pack our bags and head back to the coast. What do you say Sylvia?"

Mrs Vegas smiled in agreement. "We won't be staying if our boys don't like it here Aunt Bessie. You know that."

"Yes darling," Aunt Bessie said, patting her niece's hand like she used to when Mrs Vegas was a girl. "I know."

After clearing the table, his Aunt Bessie said her goodnights and began climbing the stairs to the guest room, but not before she winked at Stevie when no-one was watching. Shortly afterwards, Stevie too said goodnight to his parents.

As he tiptoed past his Aunt's room, Stevie projected his thoughts. "What time are we leaving tonight?" His Aunt answered that he should be ready by 11pm and he was to meet her downstairs in the front garden with his skateboard. She also added that he should dress warmly and wear dark colors to blend with the nightfall.

At precisely 11pm Stevie was ready. They didn't dare speak until they had just about traversed the gravel drive to the main road and were out of earshot of the bungalow.

"Are you alright?" his Aunt said, as they stepped as softly as they could on the pebbly driveway.

Stevie nodded, a half smile on his face. "But Aunt Bessie don't you think it's time to tell me where we are going?"

They came to the main road and his Aunt pointed to the Barron estate about half a mile up the road. "There," she said.

"What!" Stevie exclaimed. "We'll be caught for sure. We can't just go up to the Barron's front gate and say, let us in...I'm after a couple of stones."

"Now Stevie, don't be silly. Of course we are not going to do that. No, I have a better plan. You know the deep culvert at the side of the estate?"

"Uh? Oh, yes...that one. I've always thought it would be fun to try and skate on it." Stevie became aware of the skateboard under his arm and suddenly his Aunt's request that he bring his skateboard made all the sense in the world.

"You want me to jump the wall using the culvert?" he said, a look of pure astonishment in his face. Yet there was some part of him that was prepared to believe it could be done.

His Aunt's face filled with the mischievous smile she had worn earlier that evening. "Absolutely, and I have no doubt you will pull it off. You see Stevie, you need to because that is the only way you can unlock the side gate and let me into the estate. We need to find the Barron crypt once we are inside the grounds. That is where Chris Barron will have hidden the stones - in the most secure place he can. A place that would never be in danger of being burgled and that would never get visitors - safe and away from prying eyes."

They were nearly to the culvert which bordered the east wall of the estate. "You amaze me Aunt Bessie. How do you know all this?"

"We Illuminators have our ways and means. Some of this information was passed to me by a close friend who used to work as a gardener at the estate some years ago. The rest...well...let's just say I 'tuned in' a couple of times to Chris Barron's thoughts."

Stevie marveled at his Aunt's daring and realised he had a lot to learn about being an Illuminator. They reached the culvert just as the moon decided to retreat behind a cloud. Stevie shivered in the night air.

"Never mind," his Aunt whispered in the darkness. "When in the dark, light a match I say." His Aunt pulled out what appeared to be a necklace from her pocket. It was intricately woven with small white quartz stones strung with gleaming silver. The centerpiece of the necklace was a large, white quartz stone which, to Stevie's amazement, began to glow in the dark night, illuminating the blackness with the intensity of its light. It was the most unusual object Stevie had ever seen and he instantly felt drawn to it like a cold body to the warmth of a fireside.

"I want you to have this Stevie," she said, placing it over his head, and around his neck. The warmth and brightness of its glow lit the area around him with their intensity. "This will not only light your way in dark times, but will protect you from the power of the cursed stones."

"But Aunt Bessie," Stevie began to protest. "What about you?"

His Aunt reached into her other pocket and pulled out a larger stone that also glowed white against the blackness of the night. "All Illuminators carry their own stone to protect them. I have been keeping the necklace for you ever since you were born and I saw the mark of the Illuminator on your shoulder. The necklace Stevie was always destined for your possession."

The necklace felt warm against his skin and, in an odd way, reassured Stevie that all would be well. "I feel safe with it on," he whispered. "And not in the slightest bit scared."

"I don't ever want you to be scared of anything Stevie," his Aunt said, giving his arm a comforting pat. "While-ever you have the necklace on, the affects of evil will be diminished on you - but there is always a need for caution...and bravery...in this world."

Stevie nodded understanding her meaning. "I know Aunt Bessie. I'm never sure about whether I will make a skating jump or not but I imagine myself making a perfect landing, and mostly I do."

"That's all we can do darling, and I believe the power of those positive thoughts often carries us through. Now imagine you make the culvert jump and land safely on the wall."

Stevie placed his skateboard at the top of the culvert, put on his protective gear which he had earlier put in his rucksack, and went through his usual preparations before a major jump. He imagined flying through the air with perfect timing to land on the estate's wall. He pushed off on his skateboard and dropped into the culvert, gathering speed as he reached the bottom to propel himself up the other side. The momentum he gathered shot him into the air and he caught sight of the wall. Within an instant he knew he didn't have enough air to make the jump and he turned his board instead and dropped smoothly back into the culvert.

Without looking at his Aunt, he gathered speed for his second attempt, only this time pushing off a little harder. As he shot into the air for a second time, he imagined making the jump and the feel of his feet touching the rim of the estate wall. Within seconds his feet felt the concrete rim he had been imagining and he kicked up his skateboard, catching it deftly with one hand as his feet stabilised on the wall. He grinned triumphantly down at his Aunt.

However his Aunt had no time for congratulations and with urgency in her voice, called up to Stevie. "There should be a lattice on the other side of the wall. I want you to carefully climb down it and let me in the side gate. I can't open it myself as I need to conserve all my energy for the task ahead."

Following his Aunt's instructions, it wasn't long before Stevie shimmied down the garden wall and found the side gate. A relieved Aunt Bessie greeted him. Once they were both safely in the grounds, his Aunt searched the darkness of the landscaped grounds for the family crypt. "There," she whispered, pointing to the north east end of the grounds. "I can just make it out."

Stevie looked as best he could through the darkness, grateful for the comforting feel of the white stone necklace against his skin. Looming ahead in the darkness was the Barron's family crypt. He took a step towards the crypt but immediately began to feel blackness as thick as ink swirling through the air around him. It pulsated in waves thundering out from the crypt. He shivered in the night air, taking a deep breath and steeling himself against the pressing feeling that was beginning to grip his chest. His Aunt touched his shoulder reassuringly and he felt a lightness encircle him. Step by step they made their way to the front entrance.

It was only when they reached the huge stone doors that Stevie realised they had absolutely no way of getting into the crypt. "I might have been able to skate well enough to let us into the grounds," he whispered to his Aunt. "But there is no way I can help with this."

His aunt smiled, the moonlight lighting her face. Stevie could see she was both excited and anxious at the challenge ahead. "Don't worry Stevie," she said, pushing her fears away and taking a deep breath. "It's my turn to produce an ace from my sleeve and I...well...I think I have enough energy to do this."

Stevie looked puzzled.

"Now, no questions please. I need to concentrate."

Aunt Bessie closed her eyes and Stevie became more and more puzzled at what might happen next. He felt the air change from the engulfing blackness to something else...it was like an electrical current ran through the night and it began to build, pushing the negative energy back. As it built in intensity you could almost hear the low hum of its current growing louder, as though it was about to arc in mid air.

Breathing deeply with the effort of her conjuring, his Aunt took the stone from her pocket and Stevie saw it was glowing with the whitest, most brilliant light he had ever seen. Simultaneously, his own necklace began to glow and pulsate, though far less brilliant than Aunt Bessie's stone. All around him the air was exploding with massive currents of energy. As it reached a crescendo, the door of the crypt burst open. His Aunt stumbled backwards with the force and Stevie caught her just in time to prevent her fall.

"Quickly," she urged, between shallow breaths. "We do not have much time to get the cursed stones. Chris Barron will have felt my little trick from Lake View and is, at this very moment, making his excuses to his guests in order to return speedily to Smithson."

Stevie supported his Aunt as they entered the crypt, the light of their stones illuminating their way. At the centre of the crypt a pedestal held what appeared to be a large black object. It was surrounded by shards of black aura shooting and spiking into the air, as if it was a living thing. Stevie felt its energy - heavy, menacing and all engulfing. He knew instinctively that whatever it was, it was pure evil and he drew as far away from it as he possibly could.

"It's alright Stevie," his aunt said, speaking calmly to reassure him. "It cannot harm you while-ever you are wearing your necklace, though it would be foolhardy to touch a cursed stone."

"A stone? How can a simple stone be so...so evil," he said, shivering despite his jacket.

"Remember Stevie, it has been carrying the original Shadowcasters spells for centuries - its energy has built up over time. It is no ordinary stone."

"But Aunt Bessie if we can't touch the stone, how can we remove it from the crypt?"

His Aunt smiled, despite their dim, dank surroundings, and pulled a sheath of pure white silk from her pocket. "This will help. It is the only material on earth that can contain the stone's negative energies."

She wrapped the large stone in the silk, struggling under its weight. As soon as the silk encircled the stone, Stevie felt its energy lessen considerably. Only a faint seed of evil remained as long as the stone was encircled by the purity of the silk.

"Now, quickly young man," his Aunt said, placing the stone in his rucksack and propelling him out of the crypt. "We need to be away from this place before Chris Barron returns...or we are discovered. Everything depends on it."

They half ran, half stumbled, through the dark night, their stones lighting the way across the unfamiliar grounds. It wasn't until they were outside the gate, over the culvert and deep within the woods that they stopped to draw breath. Leaning against the trunk of the tree they stopped, little wisps of mist forming in the night air with each deep breath they took.

"We can rest here a minute...but not for long. Even now...there is danger...great danger," his Aunt said between deep breaths. "Chris Barron can sense the location of his stone despite the protective silk and we must dispose of it quickly Stevie, somewhere where Chris Barron will never find it."

"But where Aunt Bessie?" he said, shifting the heavy weight of his rucksack more evenly on his back and wishing that wherever they were to dispose of it, would be nearby. He didn't like being so close to the stone and could not get an image of red, angry eyes from his mind. While he didn't fully understand the source of the Shadowcasters' powers, he knew that it was not human. He shuddered against the night air. "Aunt Bessie, we need to hurry where-ever we are going."

"I know Stevie. Let's keep moving. We are going to the river." His Aunt began to move off again quickly, despite her years, stepping deftly through the forest's undergrowth like someone 20 years younger. Stevie admired her energy and, ignoring the heaviness on his back and the images of the red inhumane eyes, followed quickly from behind.

"I have made preparations to hide the stone within the river's deep waters. It will be lost to the Barrons forever...unless they plan on diving and searching the entire riverbed to find it."

Stevie remembered his geography. Many tributaries fed the Katonga River and it eventually led out to sea. It was the third largest river in the state. His Aunt was right; once in the river the stone would never be found.

They quickened their pace, and half-running reaching the river's bank where Stevie had met Chipara. It seemed a lifetime ago, given the events of the past few hours.

Aunt Bessie steadied herself at the water's edge. Stevie could hear the rushing of the current in the darkness and felt the chill of the night off the cold water.

His aunt pulled a large metal box from her rucksack. Like the stone it was heavy and, struggling with its weight, she set it down on the bank. She took the stone from Stevie's bag and leaving the protective silk wrapping intact, placed it within the metal box, slamming the lid tightly shut and locking it securely.

As if reading Stevie's thoughts, his Aunt said: "The metal box and the silk will be enough to stop the signal the stone is sending out to Chris Barron and once we deposit it in the river, he will never be able to locate it."

She pointed to the nearby bush straddling the water's edge. "There is a small rowboat tethered to the bush. We will need to take the box and stone out to the middle of the river and caste it in. But we need to hurry; every second is critical."

Stevie was used to the water, often fishing with his dad at Valley Dale. Within a second he had loosened the boat from its temporary mooring and, between he and his Aunt, managed to get the metal box with its menacing contents inside the boat. Aunt Bessie climbed in and Stevie began to row with all his strength, conscious of finishing their task and of the ever present danger from Chris Barron.

When they reached the middle of the river, Stevie let the boat drift.

"Here, this will do perfectly," his Aunt said, attempting to lift the box, but it was heavy and she strained under its weight. They were both tiring as the enormity of the night's task began to take its toll.

"Let me help," Stevie said, summoning the last of his strength and getting into position to lift one side of the box while his Aunt lifted the other. With a mighty heave they caste the box over the side. The heavy metal acted as a weight and the dark, swirling waters of the Katonga soon immersed their burden, so that it sank quickly and disappeared entirely from their view.

Stevie flopped back into the boat with sheer relief and exhaustion. Their task had been accomplished. The cursed stone would never be found and the Barron's power was diminished, or so he thought.

His Aunt sank back into the boat too - the night had taken its toll on her. Stevie rowed quickly for the shore and, helping his Aunt out of the boat, let go of the boat rope, knowing it would soon drift downstream. If Barron were to find it, it would be a long way from where they had thrown the cursed stone into the river.

Aunt Bessie sat down by the water's edge, breathing heavily. It was only then that Stevie fully realised she had accomplished more in that evening than could be expected of an elderly women in her 60s.

He sat down beside her. "I know we need to keep moving Aunt Bessie but you need to rest for a minute."

She shook her head. "No Stevie, we must get home. Chris Barron has reached his estate and will follow our trail to the river. We must be in the safety of our bungalow where I can caste an illumination spell over the bungalow. He will not enter it tonight, but I fear he will visit us tomorrow in the light of a new day."

Stevie helped his aunt to her feet. "It doesn't matter does it? We have stopped him, haven't we?"

To his utter surprise, his Aunt shook her head. "Stevie all did not go to plan tonight despite the success in getting one of the cursed stones. You see I was expecting two cursed stones in the crypt."

"Two stones...that can't be possible...why?"

"One stone without a doubt belonged to Chris Barron, but there is another cursed stone which belongs to his son Jacob. I was expecting it to be in the crypt too but it must be kept somewhere in the house. The information I obtained was not totally accurate. In any case, we must be satisfied with at least one victory tonight Stevie."

They had reached the safety of the bungalow, with its night light leading the way through the last few metres of dark forest.

"Now up to bed and sleep if you can Stevie my boy," his aunt whispered as they climbed the stairs. "Not a word to anyone."

Stevie nodded, careful not disturb the sleeping Vegas family. As he reached his bed he realised how exhausted he was. He would sleep soundly however his sleep was anything but sound that night. All night he dreamt of another cursed stone and he knew that without this piece of the puzzle the Barron's power was not destroyed. In his sleeplessness he reached for his necklace and took a small measure of comfort from its warm glow against the chill which threatened to engulf the Vegas bungalow.

But the chill which forewarned of events to come only penetrated slightly that night, held back by Aunt Bessie's protective spell that would last only until daylight.

CHAPTER 11 - THE BARRON'S WRATH

Stevie woke sharply to the pounding on the front door. It startled him so much that he sat bolt upright and was wide awake despite only getting a few hours sleep. Throwing on his usual black jeans and long sleeved T, he hurried downstairs. His Aunt and his Dad were talking to Chris Barron at the front door.

Before he had even reached the foyer, Stevie felt the anger pulsating from Barron like fists punching him hard in the chest. He was trying hard to hide his discomfort from his dad, but he could see Barron's dark aura growing blacker by the minute. It was shooting invisible black shards into the air around his father and his aunt, like black ash spewing out of a volcano ready to erupt. Stevie noticed his aunt was deathly pale with the effort of holding back the negative energy that was trying to consume the house. Blissfully ignorant of last night's events, his father appeared confused by Chris Barron's early morning visit.

"No I'm sorry Chris, we definitely can't help you - we've not seen anyone come and go from the estate, last night or this morning," his dad said. "In fact, we spent a quiet family evening at home and then we all had an early night. Isn't that right Aunt Bessie?"

Stevie, who was nearly to the bottom of the stairs, drew in his breath and held it. How on earth could his aunt answer that question?

His aunt drew her dressing gown around her and Stevie noticed her features were grim. "As you can see Mr Barron from my night attire at this early hour of the morning, sleep has been, and is, the only thing on my mind. In fact I was sleeping soundly when your...knock...woke me."

Barron could hardly contain himself and Stevie noticed his lips were like a thin line across his flushed face. His eyes hid the obvious hatred he felt for Aunt Bessie.

"Pardon me for my intrusion, Mrs..."

Stevie's dad intervened. "It's Miss Orion actuall..."

"Miss Orion, but I have just been robbed of a very valuable artifact from my estate. It was priceless; its value inestimable. It is a very strong priority that I get to the bottom of the theft. As the Vegas bungalow is the closest house to the estate, it is understandable that I should make this my first stop in my investigations."

His aunt stepped backwards, just a little, as if thrown off guard by the invisible force of Barron's icy tone.

His dad tried to intervene again. "Chris, as I've said already we haven't witnessed anything unusual..."

His father was unable to finish his sentence as Barron caught sight of Stevie on the staircase. Instantaneously, Stevie felt the full force of Barron's mind probing his. Stevie deliberately concentrated on the vase of flowers in the foyer, his hand going instinctively to the necklace in his pocket. Closing his hand around it, he felt a white light surge through him, shielding him from Barron's gaze.

A look of surprise momentarily flashed across Chris Barron's angry face. Undeterred, he pressed on. "As Stevie is here, you won't mind Alexander if I asked him a few questions."

It was more of a statement than a question and Mr Vegas opened the door fully, reluctantly inviting the clearly upset Chris Barron inside." Of course not. That is fine, though Stevie knows no more than we do. As I said, we spent a quiet family night indoors."

Without looking at his aunt, Stevie descended the last of the stairs and took a seat in the lounge room next to his father. He continued to keep his mind blank, his fingers encircling his illuminator stone necklace. However he noticed the black shards shooting out of Chris Barron's aura had begun to subside.

Chris Barron sat down on the nearby chair. "I am sure you know nothing about the events last night Stevie," he said in his most polite, almost seductive tone - the tone he had previously used on the Vegas family in Valley Dale. He smiled engagingly at Stevie.

Stevie refused to return his smile and sat resolutely in his chair. He did not trust Barron. He knew him for what he was, a liar and a manipulator. Nevertheless, Barron continued with his pretence." As I was saying, someone has gained entry to my estate and taken a priceless artifact that was centuries old and had been in handed down through my ancestors to the present day. It is imperative that I get it back."

Stevie brushed his untidy fringe from his face, realising he must look like he had just got out of bed. Again, he steeled his mind for Barron's probe, but it did not come. Instead Barron's thoughts penetrated his mind:

"I know that you have information about what occurred last night Stevie. I am not stupid and fooled by your aunt's stories. You see, I am not going to make a scene here, in front of your dad. Instead, I am offering you a deal. Give me the information I desire and no harm will befall you or your family."

Alarmed Stevie looked straight at his aunt, but Barron's thoughts cut off any chance of assistance from his Aunt Bessie. It was like only he and Barron were in the room.

"I don't know what you are talking about...I was asleep..." Stevie thought.

Barron's onslaught continued. "Spare me your child-like stories. I am no fool. Your old aunt sitting next to us is no more innocent than you. I sense your involvement and hers in the events of last night. I am just not clear what that involvement is. But rest assured I will get to the bottom of it."

Just as quickly as the mind onslaught began, it stopped. Barron, instead, spoke directly to him. His tone was soft and almost parental-like. "Well Stevie, please forgive me my bad temper, but as you can see I am quite upset about being robbed of one of my most treasured possessions. Did you see anything last night that was unusual?" He leant over and touched Stevie's hand. At that moment it was if Barron had given him a truth serum. Try as he might to blank out the thoughts of the previous night, Stevie could not help but think of his daring skateboard trick as it was the most unusual stunt he had ever pulled on a skateboard to date.

Barron sat back in his chair, a satisfied smile creasing the corners of his thin lips. He turned to Aunt Bessie, locking his gaze with hers. "We are not sure how the intruders gained entry to the estate, but we are beginning to piece together the puzzle and I know it won't be too long before we solve this particular mystery and the thieves will be punished for their crime."

Aunt Bessie stood up, her gaze never wavering for a moment." Mr Barron, I hope you find your intruders - they must have been very clever indeed to gain entry to your estate without detection. As I have not yet dressed and my nephew really does need to get to back to bed, please excuse us."

"Thank you for your hospitality," Barron said, turning to Stevie's dad who, by this time, was looking even more confused than before.

As he got to the door, he stopped. "Oh, and Stevie, remember, if you think of anything that would assist me in my investigations, please let me know. It will save a lot of time and possibly trouble if I were to locate the missing artifact...sooner rather than later."

Stevie did not reply, only nodded at Barron before his father closed the front door.

"My goodness," Mr Vegas said, sounding perplexed. "What an odd visit. I've never seen this side of Chris Barron, but I could swear he sounded threatening."

Stevie smiled half-heartedly at his aunt and then at his dad. "His lost treasure must be very valuable to him."

His Aunt nodded. "Well Alexander, I have to say I found him a most unpleasant man - so unpleasant, I will have to go and lie down."

Stevie watched his Aunt disappear upstairs. Suddenly he was overcome with tiredness. Luckily, it was a pupil free day and he did not have to attend school. "I think I will go back to bed for a while if that is alright dad."

His father nodded, yawning widely. "That's not a bad idea Stevie."

Once upstairs he knocked quietly on his aunt's door. "Come in Stevie," she whispered. Stevie noticed she had dressed and was looking anything but tired now they were on their own.

"There's no need to tell me," she said. "I know, Barron tried a mind probe and I also know you resisted. Good boy," she said, giving him a familiar pat on the arm.

"But Aunt Bessie, didn't you pick up that he used telepathy on me and threatened to harm my family if I didn't tell him what I know...and there's something else...I couldn't help but think of my skateboarding over the culvert and I think he picked up on that image. I know he's putting two and two together."

Sitting down on the bed, his Aunt patted a welcoming space beside her. "Come sit awhile and I'll let you in on a little secret. As much as Chris Barron might try his tricks on you, you are more than a match for him. His actions this morning were that of a desperate man. If he had his cursed stone, it would have been a different story, and he would have drawn the information he needed from you within a matter of seconds."

Stevie's eyes widened with doubt. "And that's not all Stevie," his Aunt continued. "No harm will befall you while I'm here."

Stevie smiled, albeit reluctantly. He wanted to believe his aunt but he couldn't shake the feeling Barron had an ace up his sleeve they knew nothing about. His intuition was sending him a strong warning and, despite his Aunt Bessie's reassurances, he felt something was very wrong.

CHAPTER 12 - TROUBLE FOR JEM

It was one of those brilliantly sunny mornings when his dad dropped the Vegas brothers off at Smithson High. The schoolyard was abuzz with activity and Stevie felt almost normal as he made his way through the crowded corridors to class. He gave Jem a wink as he left him in front of the Year 5 classroom, but Jem didn't return Stevie's good humor. He was far too pre-occupied these days, Stevie thought and definitely not his usual self. Stevie made a mental note to take the soccer ball down to the river and kick it round - also a good opportunity for a brother to brother talk.

As he entered the classroom, he noticed Principal Hawker was teaching and not his usual teacher Miss Robertson. Feeling the penetrating glare of the principal on his back, he made his way to his seat and sat down as quietly as he could. He was in no mood for a tussle with the principal, wanting only to be as anonymous as he could for the next few weeks until the break in at the Barron estate became old news.

The events of the past week or so had left Stevie's head spinning. He was still trying to compute all he'd learned. He had fired what seemed to be millions of questions at Aunt Bessie about Illuminators and now knew that he was not alone in his ability to read minds, sense events before they occurred and, in very rare circumstances, make things happen with his thoughts. He glanced around the schoolroom, his gaze stopping on Jacob Barron and his offsider McCauley. He immediately thought about Chipara's warning that there were always two sides to the coin. He knew for certain that Jacob Barron was as evilly motivated as his father and, as for McCauley, the boy had a meanness in his face common in most bullies. His blonde, shoulder length hair framed a thick-set face and ruddy complexion. He was big for his age which gave him a confidence in the schoolyard that was rarely challenged by his peers, who were usually smaller than him anyway. However, it was his eyes that struck fear into the boys he preyed upon - cold as blue steel and without a hint of emotion.

McCauley made the perfect henchman for Jacob Barron who, in contrast, was smallish and dark. Stevie knew for sure that he would rather take on McCauley any day. He knew Barron was quick and agile and secretive - you would never see the blow that came from Barron, only feel its force far too late.

Both Barron and McCauley were whispering, obviously about something important, because they were going to great lengths to make sure no-one overheard. Stevie looked up at Principal Hawker. He apparently did not notice the frantic whispering and he wondered if Jacob Barron got special treatment. He suspected he did, given the principal's black aura almost mirrored the Barrons.

The double English and then History classes all proceeded slowly for Stevie and he was relieved when the recess buzzer sounded throughout the school's corridors. He noticed Barron and McCauley just about ran out of the classroom. Stevie spied Tom Lee as he was leaving.

"What gives with Barron and McCauley?" Stevie asked. Of all the kids at Smithson High, Tom was probably the only one Stevie trusted. He made a mental note to invite him over on the weekend. It might also be good for Jem if he introduced him to Tom, as he knew Tom liked to play soccer.

Tom gave him a welcoming smile. "Hi Stevie, yeah...not sure about those two but I did hear something big was on today - some kid they've been bullying has accepted a dare to climb up onto the science block roof."

Stevie's eyes widened. "But the science block is a three story building. It's madness to climb that."

Tom agreed. "I suppose the kid felt he had to do it - backing down with those two is rarely an option."

Stevie felt the panic begin in the pit of his stomach. He didn't know precisely why but an image of Jem's angry, sullen face loomed large in his mind. The feeling he had after Chris Barron had left yesterday that something was dreadfully wrong returned. Before he could stop and explain his turmoil to Tom, he turned on his heel and sped towards the science block.

"Hey wait up," Tom yelled after him. "What's the matter...wait up..."

The end of Tom's sentence was drowned out by the wind whistling past him as he ran as fast as his feet could carry him. He could see the crowd gathered up ahead and he slowed down, pushing through them to the front. Without wanting to but knowing he must, Stevie looked up. He didn't have to be told. He knew. Climbing the red brick science block and using the drainpipe as a makeshift ladder, Jem had already reached the first storey. Directly below him, Jacob Barron and McCauley yelled up to him.

"Go on chicken, up you go," yelled McCauley triumphantly.

"Your feet better not touch the ground before you get to that third storey or we'll beat the living hell out you," Barron shouted.

Jem kept climbing, deftly and expertly, but his small figure inching higher and higher revealed the true extent of the danger - one wrong footing, a misplaced hand on a ledge, a crisis in confidence and he would plummet to certain injury or worse.

Stevie had to act. Somehow but how! He looked from side to side but could see nothing at first. He ran over to Barron, hardly able to contain himself.

"You scumbag. You low piece of garbage...I swear I'll..." Stevie hadn't finished his sentence before McCauley took a swipe at him. Ducking at the last minute, McCauley just about fell over from the force of his own empty punch. Barron had more luck and punched Stevie hard in the stomach, sending him to the ground on his knees, winding him. It took all of Stevie's willpower not to pass out from the hit. He shook his head from side to side, as if to get rid of the grogginess that threatened to engulf his consciousness. Getting to his feet and trying to catch his breath, he turned to the crowd.

"Someone!" he yelled desperately. "Help my brother." Their faces were a blur but he knew there was fear in them. They did not want to take on Jacob Barron or McCauley and mark themselves for the rest of their time at Smithson High as potential victims of the bullies. He waited, hoping, but no-one stepped forward.

Stevie took a deep breath and centred his thoughts. He turned to the crowd again knowing that he could not save Jem and fight off McCauley and Barron at the same time. He searched for Tom's face and projected his thoughts with as much drive and force as he could muster. "Get the ladder from the tool shed on our right, please, hurry, it's Jem's only chance. The ladder in the tool shed...HURRY."

Stevie didn't know if his thought projection would work on Tom. All he could do was hope. He turned back to Barron and McCauley who were laughing at him. McCauley yelled up to Jem.

"Come on squirt, my old mother could go faster than you."

Stevie noticed Jem quicken his pace and then stumble, his foot missing the ledge momentarily. He knew every second that he didn't help Jem counted and could mean the difference between his brother plummeting to the ground or surviving the climb.

He turned back to Barron and with the full force of his mind, imagined Barron flying against the wall of the science block. He mustered all his anger and indignation in that thought and pushed it outward like a wave towards an unsuspecting Barron, at the same time stepping closer to him. Jacob Barron was immediately flung backwards, hitting the wall and falling to the ground, but to the watching crowd it appeared as if Stevie had pushed him. McCauley took a step towards him but something in Stevie's maddened, desperate, face stopped him mid step.

At that moment Tom and one of Jem's classmates from Year 5 appeared to Stevie's right carrying a ladder.

Without turning away from Barron and McCauley, Stevie yelled to them to place the ladder directly under Jem. In the meantime Barron and McCauley were motionless, half shocked by the force of Stevie's will and the inexplicable way he had pushed Barron to the wall, without so much as lifting a finger.

Stevie used the power of his thoughts again, knowing Barron would understand. "Back away and leave and I won't use my powers again on you."

Almost instantly Barron replied: "Sure, our job's done here anyway. Try and get your brother down now Vegas!"

Without so much as a glance up at Jem, the two bullies turned on their heel and ran off, just before Principal Hawker arrived.

Stevie ignored the principal's angry expression, instead turning his full attention on Jem. The ladder fell about three feet short of him. Jem would need to climb back down the drainpipe to get to it. Stevie yelled up encouragement, but Jem seemed frozen to the spot.

"Come on Jem. You can do it. You got up there didn't you. Retrace your footholds."

Jem shook his head, yelling back down to Stevie. "I can't Stevie. I just can't." He began to cry. "I'm not you...I can't do it. I never could."

Stevie fought back his own tears. "That's not true Jemmy, come on. You can kick a soccer goal from half way up the field. I could never do that. Jem, please, we haven't got much time...retrace your steps."

To Stevie's utter relief, he could see that Jem was very slowly but surely climbing back down. Within seconds he had reached the ladder. Tom and Jem's friend held the ladder steady and Jem began to descend - all the while Stevie kept up his encouraging words. The danger, it seemed, had almost passed and some of the churn in the pit of Stevie's stomach was beginning to recede.

Jem was three quarters of the way down the ladder when his foot missed a bottom rung. "No!" Stevie yelled, running towards him hoping to somehow reverse the truly terrifying thing he knew was about to happen. As if in slow motion Jem fell, hitting the ground below. Stevie got to him in a split second. Still conscious Jem moaned and held his leg. "Stevie, it hurts bad...it hurts...my leg..."

Principal Hawker came from out of nowhere. "It's ok, everyone...please go back to your home rooms." He reached inside his coat and pulled out his mobile phone, dialing 999. "Help is on its way."

Jem tried hard not to cry. "I did it for you Stevie...I did. They said they'd hurt you if I didn't do it...the dare...Stevie my leg, it hurts..."

Stevie took his jacket off and put it under Jem's head. "It's ok Jemmy. Don't talk; the ambulance will be here soon. No-one is going to hurt me or you...you did good up there today...very brave and better than the highest jump I've ever pulled off."

Between tears Jem managed a limp smile and nodded, his quiet sobs the only sound in the courtyard. Only Tom and one of Jem's friends remained...and Principal Hawker. Stevie glanced up at him. "Where were you Sir?" he asked. "When Jem was climbing the ladder. I could have done with a hand you know."

Principal Hawker looked angrily at Stevie. "How dare you Vegas. I was sending the crowd back to their home rooms and calling for assistance. You and your brother seemed to have managed to get yourself into this trouble on your own."

"But you saw Barron and McCauley egging Jem on." Stevie protested.

"I did no such thing; they were leaving as I arrived. But I will question them. If they have had anything to do with today's events, they will be punished."

Stevie doubted Principal Hawker would ever question the son of his close friend and associate Chris Barron, any more than Stevie would ever stay in the same room as Chris Barron again.

As sure as the sun rises every morning Stevie knew Chris Barron had something to do with Jem's fall and was making good his threat of yesterday that if Stevie didn't tell him what he knew, something bad would happen to either him or his family.

He faced Principal Hawker squarely, his hand never leaving Jem's. "I don't care what you say; this town, this school, the Barrons and you...you are all responsible for what's happened today...I know it."

At that moment the whir of the ambulance siren reached Stevie's ears. "It's ok Jemmy," he said, gently brushing Jem's blonde hair away from his eyes which were creased with pain. "Everything is going to be alright; you'll see."

Stevie reluctantly backed away from his brother as the ambulance officers went to work, splinting Jem's leg and gently lifting him onto the stretcher.

"Looks like a broken leg," the paramedic radioed into the hospital.

Stevie watched while his brother's small face disappeared from view, though Jem maintained a small smile back at Stevie until the ambulance doors shut. They would take him to Smithson General and Stevie would follow with Principal Hawker. His parents would meet them at the hospital.

As the ambulance pulled away, Stevie noticed a small crowd had gathered again. He caught sight of Jacob Barron out of the corner of his eye. He marched up to him before

Principal Hawker had a chance to grab him. With his face inches away from a smiling Barron, Stevie said through clenched teeth: "You and me...tomorrow night at the skate park...let's finish this!"

Barron's eyes flashed with triumph. "I thought you would never ask Vegas. I've been waiting for this chance for some time now. No more stepping around it; no more making out our families are friends. It's me and you now and you better watch out because you are not walking away from this one."

"It's you who should remember who has the power here," Stevie shouted, not caring who was listening.

Stevie felt a surge of hatred begin in the soles of his feet and travel along his spine like an electrical current. His head almost exploded with the force of his fury. Only a small voice deep inside him prevented him from projecting his rage toward Jacob Barron who, feeling the surge of energy emanating from Stevie, took a step back, half faltering for a second before regaining his confidence.

The small voice inside Stevie's head grew louder and the measured tone of Chipara urging him to use his power wisely broke through the dark rage that threatened to engulf Stevie. He calmed himself and when he spoke his voice was icy: "Tomorrow night...a test of skating skill alone...no mind tricks."

Barron nodded, his eyes gleaming. "Of course Vegas. Your skating skill against mine. No tricks."

CHAPTER 13 - SKATE OFF

Stevie discarded his usual black jeans, instead reaching for the new pair of Fatigues his mum had purchased for him yesterday. Pulling his black and white T on and lacing his skater shoes tight with a double knot, he was almost ready to go. He had convinced his mum and dad to drop him at Skateopia for a two hour practice session. They had agreed, although somewhat reluctantly, because they thought it might take his mind off Jem.

Jem was in Smithson General, having just come through an operation to insert a pin in his shattered leg. He would be alright with time the doctors said and he would not have a limp, but his baseball days were behind him at least for a season. Stevie felt the anger surge within him every time he thought of Jem's ashen face, almost bloodless against the whiteness of the hospital linen. His blue eyes clouded with pain...

Stevie reached for Jem's favorite baseball cap which he had retrieved from Jem's room earlier that night. He didn't normally wear caps, preferring the feel of the wind in his hair as he skated, but tonight was different. It was comforting to have something of Jem's. Stevie put the cap to his face, taking in the familiar smell of Jem. He gritted his teeth. Barron would pay dearly for what he'd done.

A soft knock at his bedroom door roused Stevie from his thoughts. Aunt Bessie peeped around the corner. "Can I come in?" she said, just a little uncertainly.

"Of course you can," Stevie answered, giving her a half smile. Like the rest of the Vegas family, Aunt Bessie was reeling from the news of Jem's accident.

Sitting down at his desk, Stevie noticed his aunt looked tired. "Try not to worry Aunt Bessie," he said reassuringly, "Jem will be ok."

"It's not Jem I'm worried about Stevie, it's you."

"Me?" Stevie said.

"Yes," his aunt answered. "Jem will be fine in time but you...I can't believe you are going to take Jacob Barron on when you know he still has a cursed stone. You don't know what you are going up against."

Ignoring his aunt momentarily, Stevie put Jem's baseball cap firmly on, tilting it slightly to one side - just how Jem would have worn it. He reached into his pocket and pulled out his Illuminator stone which was pulsating with a low white light.

"You see Aunt Bessie? I don't need to worry about Jacob Barron's cursed stone. I have my Illuminator stone for protection and a whole lot of skill Jacob Barron doesn't have on a skateboard. What's more I have the added motivation of skating for Jem. I can't change the way things turned out yesterday, but I can even the score and stand up to Barron...show him and everybody else that bullies don't win in the end."

His aunt sighed. "I know your intentions are good Stevie, but what you are doing is dangerous." She studied him closely in the half-light of the bedroom. "You're determined to do this?" He nodded and she knew in that moment she was powerless to change his mind. "Then give me a minute... I'll need to put a protective shield around you."

Stevie began to protest. "There's no need...really..."

"Oh, but there is," his aunt replied, ignoring his pleas. "You have no idea how much the Barrons will want to win tonight and to be 'seen' to win." She closed her eyes tightly and Stevie immediately felt a warm rush of energy surge through him and around him.

He smiled at his aunt. "Thanks," he said simply, reaching for his rucksack. "Wish me luck."

"You have it Stevie and remember, when it gets rough out there, and it will, concentrate on why you are skating, not on the Barrons or what they have done, but the skill and competition involved in your skate off."

Stevie looked slightly puzzled. "Sure," he said, without knowing quite what his aunt meant. "I'll remember. It's for Jem."

With a wink he was gone and she heard the sound of the Ford Territory's engine kick into life in the garage below. She hoped against all hope that the lesson coming to Stevie would end well. She put her head down and began to project positive thoughts into the universe and to strengthen the protective shield she had placed around her nephew - it was all she could do now. The rest was up to Stevie.

His mum drove quickly to Skateopia, not wanting to miss visiting hours at the hospital. Kissing him rather absent-mindedly, she reminded him she would be back in two hours. As the Ford Territory pulled out of the park's front gate, Stevie felt momentarily alone, until he heard a familiar voice.

"Hey Vegas, all ready for the biggest skating test of your life?" Stevie turned around to see the friendly face of Tom Lee.

"Yep," he said, rather too confidently. Up ahead a crowd was gathering, mostly Jacob Barron's mob, but a few kids who had been bullied over the years by Barron and McCauley were standing to one side of the Barron supporters. Stevie also picked out McCauley in the crowd and noticed that he wasn't quite as cocky as he had been yesterday. On the other hand, Jacob Barron seemed to have doubled his nerve. Stevie watched on as he strutted from one side of the half-pipe to the next, waving his arms in the air in a premature victory salute. When Stevie climbed the ladder to stand on the half-pipe's ledge, Barron's supporters booed and jeered. Only the voice of Tom Lee and a handful of others cheered him on, their show of support almost drowning out before it reached him. Nevertheless, he waved confidently down to them.

On the ledge he paused momentarily to steady his nerves which, despite himself, were swirling in the pit of his stomach. He pulled out his Illuminator stone and put the necklace on. It felt warm and comforting on his chest. Barron, a menacing grin distorting his features, stepped closer to him.

"How do you want to do this Vegas - let the crowd decide?" Without looking at him, Stevie nodded.

"You know you're a dead man walking tonight Vegas." Barron jeered at him. "You won't get up from this one."

Stevie felt a rush of air almost knock him off the ledge. "That's just for starters," Barron said, the grin never leaving his face. "You see I have something in my pocket that is more powerful than that lame excuse for a stone you have around your neck. Remember, it's the force of the power that counts and tonight I've got you outgunned."

With that Barron dropped in, gathering speed on his board. His momentum increased and Stevie watched in awe as he executed an almost perfect 360, finishing with a Kickflip. The crowd went wild and Stevie knew Barron would be a hard act to follow, with or without a cursed stone.

He dropped his board in mentally imagining the double somersault he was about to try and pull off. He took four or five runs to get his momentum up and with a final burst of will and trust that he'd pulled off enough air to complete the double turn he flew skyward, bending his body and holding onto his board. It was like the world was spinning and Stevie could see the half-pipe coming quickly into view. Rather than completing his second 360, he modified it into a 180 at the last minute. The trick worked and despite themselves the crowd let out a roar. Landing squarely on the edge of the half-pipe, Stevie could see the grin disappear from Barron's face.

"Right," Barron yelled above the roar. "We go together! One, two..." He dropped in to the half-pipe, taking Stevie by surprise, but Stevie caught himself and followed behind in a split second. Their eyes locked as they gathered momentum for their stunts and Stevie not only saw, but felt the venom coming from the cursed stone. He was just about to execute a Kickflip when he was hit by a rush of wind which threatened his balance. He wavered on the board trying to regain his footing for just a minute before freefalling and hitting the hard surface of the half-pipe. His board tumbled down, ricocheting off the half-pipe as it came to land alongside Stevie with a crash. Momentarily everything blacked out, but Stevie could still hear Tom Lee's voice yelling above the Barron supporters and the dense fog that gripped his senses. "Get up Stevie, get up. Don't let him win."

The image of Tom and then of Jem flashed quickly into Stevie's mind. He felt the power of his Illuminator stone against his chest surging through him in great waves of light. As he lay there, in that split second before he would get up, Stevie knew that taking a stand and fighting for what was right was the only thing that prevented evil's spread. He also knew that if he didn't get up he would never skate again.

With an immense effort he pushed through the dense fog that was overpowering him. He began to breathe heavily, drawing the oxygen from the night air into his lungs. In the midst of his struggle he could hear Barron's hysterical laugh and it spurred him onwards. He would not let Barron win tonight.

Despite the pain in his elbows and his knees he got steadily to his feet, a little wobbly at first. The crowd fell into a deathly silence in utter disbelief that Stevie, who was clearly fighting for consciousness a minute ago, could get up from the fall. Barron, who was skating his victory laps, suddenly stopped. "You...you...can't be...the stone...I saw you fall...this is not supposed to happen."

Stevie skated up to him his face barely an inch away from Barron's. "I don't lay down that easily. One more trick and the winner is decided."

Barron's eyes flicked invisible daggers at him and Stevie felt the pure evil force of the stone in Barron's possession directed solely at him. But he was fearless. Stevie now knew that whatever the outcome tonight he had already proved a point - it was possible to stand up to bullies no matter how badly the odds were stacked against you. In out-performing Jacob Barron and getting up after the cowardly trick with the cursed stone, Stevie had revealed Barron for who he was and had given hope to the many boys that had been victims in the past. He knew they would now have the courage to fight against bullies in the future.

He turned his attention back to Barron who was about to drop in. "I'm going to pull off a 900," Barron yelled to Stevie.

"No," Stevie shouted. "You can't possibly. It's only ever been done once. Don't be a fool."

Barron pulled out his stone. "You're forgetting about this aren't you? I'm not stupid. I know when to stack the deck." With a scream to the crowd below, Barron pushed off making his run several times to gain momentum and enough air to complete the spins needed for the 900.

Back and forth he skated, and the crowd held its breath. At his last run Stevie could see Barron's hand clasp his stone and he felt the uprush of the waves of dark energy pulsate through the skate ramp. Stevie was forced to steady himself on the ledge against the power of the stone's pulsation.

As Barron flew through the air propelled by the stone's force, Stevie knew he had completely overshot the ramp. Attempting his spins, Barron realised too late he was about to tumble over the ramp's edge but he was powerless to stop his trick in midair. Fear replaced the confidence in his face and Stevie watched in horror as Jacob Barron hit the ground below with a sickening thud, his body crumpled and lifeless on the ground below.

CHAPTER 14 - AN ENEMY IS MADE

The cold, hard light of day drove reality home as it streamed through Stevie's bedroom window. He stirred and stretched his aching limbs. He was bruised from head to toe from the skate last night but it wasn't his outward injuries that worried him that morning.

His thoughts returned to the skate park, and to Jacob Barron's almost fatal fall. He shook his head silently as if to drive the memory away. He had watched on silently as the ambulance took Jacob away. The crowd had dispersed quickly but Tom Lee had stayed to keep him company while he waited for his mum to arrive.

"It wasn't your fault Stevie. You know that. It was either him or you and I say better it was him," Tom Lee said, looking intently at Stevie.

Stevie ran a tired hand through his hair, brushing his fringe aside. He just wanted the day to be over. "I don't know Tom. I didn't want any of this to happen. I never, never wanted anyone hurt."

"I know Stevie, but it was bound to happen wasn't it? He pushed and pushed. I could see that. He took the risk...knew what he was doing. I mean Jacob Barron was a bully and in the end he got what he deserved," Tom said.

Stevie thought he saw the Ford Territory pull into Skateopia, and he waved to his mum. He turned back to Tom. "Yeah, some would say that," Stevie said. "But you know I don't. What goes round comes round Tom, and I'm not taking any glory in Jacob's accident tonight."

His mum pulled in beside them. "Wanna lift?" Stevie said to Tom.

"Yeah, sure Stevie," he said, getting in the back. "But you know you're wrong if you're giving the Barrons a break.

They're gonna come at you now harder than ever. You shouldn't let your guard down Stevie."

He managed a half smile as he got into the car. "It's ok Tom. I'm done with them. I don't think Jacob Barron will be back skating any time soon."

And that was the problem Stevie thought, as he recalled the events and his conversation with Tom Lee. An overwhelming feeling of guilt weighed on his shoulders. If only he had done something differently, Jacob might still be walking around today.

He sighed as he noticed the green trees framing his bedroom window, and he tried to forget his conversation with Tom Lee the night before. Whatever Smithson was, despite the Barrons, it was pretty. The scene was enough to lift him, temporarily, out of his gloomy thoughts. Just maybe, he would go for a quick morning run through the woods, before anyone got up and complicated things by saying they would go with him. He pulled on his jeans and runners, threw an old T-shirt over his shoulders and reached for his baseball cap. No use moping about inside, he thought. The fresh air was just what he needed and it would take his mind off everything that had happened in Smithson - Jem's fall and Jacob Barron's accident. He needed to clear his head.

Making his way down the stairs quietly so as not to wake anyone, he was surprised when he got to the front door without alerting his Aunt Bessie, but they had stayed up late into the night talking about what had happened to Jem and at Skateopia. Aunt Bessie had done her best to stop him blaming himself. No doubt she was still sleeping. Outside the air was brisk, not exactly cold, but he did think he should have brought his jumper. He quickened his pace to try and get rid of the chill and it wasn't long before he was running in the thick woods, along the well-marked trail.

Far off he heard the squawk of an eagle and underfoot the leaves and branches that lay across the path made a crackling noise as he ran. He concentrated on the sounds of the woods, glad to feel the physical-ness of his body. He really didn't want to think about the accident, the cursed stones, and the Shadowcasters anymore. For just a short while he wanted to be a normal 12 year old boy, going for a run and testing his pace in the forest.

He ran until he tired himself out, and until he lost any thought about Illuminators or Shadowcasters. He could feel the cool air of the forest around him and smell the faint tang of the pine trees. He jumped down an embankment to the river below. Somewhere in that river Barron's cursed stone lay, its evil wrapped in Aunt Bessie's powerful magic. It would never escape and Chris Barron would never know his birthright stone again. The amulet that enhanced his Shadowcaster's powers lay not two kilometres from his estate. He sat down on the trunk of a fallen tree beside the water and caught his breathe. He watched the current take the water downstream and he wondered how long it would be before he would leave Smithson. He wondered how Jacob Barron was. They hadn't heard anything, but then again they wouldn't given Chris Barron surely knew he and Aunt Bessie had something to do with the theft of his stone.

His thoughts were interrupted by a faint crackling in the air around him, and he whirled around to see what was behind him. At first he saw nothing but as he stared into the wooded trees he saw a darkness approaching, as though whatever light penetrated the forest was being blacked out. He stood quickly just in time to steady himself from the heavy swirl of dark energy that almost knocked him off his feet. He caught his balance and immediately put his hand to his Illuminator stone. Out of instinct he imagined a bright white light surrounding him which gave him a moment of protection before Chris Barron thundered out of the clearing, and towards him.

"I thought I might catch you alone Stevie Vegas, without the protection of your aunt," he said between clenched teeth. "Alone and vulnerable and ready to tell me the truth."

Stevie backed away from him. Not frightened but aware of the anger emanating from Barron. He looked sideways at the thick bush. Behind him was the river. There appeared to be no escape.

"What do you want from me? My parents won't be very happy with your questioning me like this. Let me past. I want to go home."

Stevie attempted to push past Barron but he grabbed him by the arm. It was then Stevie saw the black, swirling pit that was inside Barron, and something else. He saw two eyes stare back at him from the darkness and he knew that Barron or whatever he was, was the most evil being he had every encountered, or perhaps ever would ever meet. He felt the familiar feeling of faintness he always felt in the presence of a Shadowcaster.

"Let me go," he said, trying to break free.

Barron's grip only tightened and he felt those eyes rise up from the darkness.

"This time you are not going anywhere young skateboarder. This time you will tell me what I need to know." Barron's voice was rising. "This time you will tell me where you put what belongs to me. This time..."

Within the blackness that threatened to engulf him, Stevie became aware of the whitest light he had ever seen beginning to form in the centre of the darkness. He heard the familiar voice of Chipara. "You will have a minute Stevie Vegas; that is all, to leave this place. Run as fast as you can, along the eastern track where you will meet your aunt. I can hold back Chris Barron and the demon within him for a few minutes. Not long. Go. Go Stevie Vegas and run as fast as you can to your freedom."

Almost immediately Barron loosened his grip, as Stevie felt an ancient energy drawn from the forest around him encircle Chris Barron like prison bars. Stevie turned around, momentarily, and saw the wrath on his face. He was hit with a thought projection: "Wherever you are Stevie Vegas I will

94

find you. Just when you feel you are safe, I will come for you. Never forget that I will be coming for you..."

Stevie threw off the thought connection and ran like the wind. He ran east as Chipara had said, through the trees, jumping over the fallen branches, and propelling himself off the grassy embankments. He followed a partial track, not knowing where he was going and with one thought in his head, to put as much distance between himself and Barron as he could...and quickly.

He felt his breath strain against his lungs until breathing caused him physical pain, but he pushed through it, intent on reaching his aunt. Just when he felt his lungs would burst he caught sight of Aunt Bessie. He ran toward her aware that the dark energy of Barron was drawing closer, pursuing him. When he was a few feet away from his aunt he ran through a white wall of light, collapsing at Aunt Bessie's feet, gulping the air around him. He looked up at his aunt who appeared to be meditating, projecting her white light of protection around them.

Chris Barron's dark energy came in waves but was unable to penetrate the white circle of protection. It enveloped it, but still couldn't break through. Aunt Bessie held firm and after what seemed like an eternity the black energy began to recede. Within moments it had disappeared. Only then did Aunt Bessie relax her guard.

"Are you alright Stevie?" she whispered, with barely enough energy to speak.

"Yes I am Aunt Bessie. Thank you for showing up. If you hadn't I don't know what would have become of me. He was angry...very angry that his cursed stone was gone and his son was injured."

Aunt Bessie sat down on the nearby log, steadying herself as she did so. Stevie was aware that the past few days had cost her.

His breathing had slowed and he put his hand again to his Illuminator stone, drawing strength from it. He put his hand over his aunt's and tried to send her some of his strength.

"Don't worry Stevie. I'm ok. Just a bit drained. It takes a bit of energy to hold a protection spell like that and particularly against someone as powerful as Chris Barron."

"But why Aunt Bessie? Why did he come for me? I would have thought he'd be at the hospital with his son."

His aunt sighed heavily. "I'm afraid Stevie he is hell bent on taking his revenge on us for what happened to his son and for the loss of his cursed stone. It's very important from now on that we protect you. You mustn't go out alone here in Smithson. Promise me Stevie you will stay close to home."

Stevie nodded. "I will Aunt Bessie but I can't stay at home forever."

She nodded. "I know my boy. I know. I just need to figure out what we do next. I will need to talk to your parents and suggest that given the skating accident with Jacob...I don't know Stevie but it is clear you can't stay in Smithson."

He looked into the dark forest surrounding them, and for the first time that afternoon was afraid.

"Do you think Chris Barron will ever stop coming after me Aunt Bessie?"

His aunt looked down at him, aware he was not yet a teenager. She bit her lip.

"I'm sorry Stevie it had to be like this. None of us wanted you in danger..."

He tightened his grip on her hand. "Don't worry about me Aunt Bessie. I've known for a long time now I am not like other boys. And now I know why. Believe me, it's far better to know than not, even if I don't want to be an Illuminator."

She smiled for a moment at his boyhood honesty. "I suppose so Stevie. I suppose so."

He helped her to his feet.

"Well I know something Stevie Vegas," she said.

"And what's that Aunt Bessie?" he said, as they walked through the clearing toward the Vegas bungalow.

"I know that you have extraordinary powers that will come in handy not once, but many times during the coming months."

Stevie stared straight ahead. "They'll come for us won't they Aunt Bessie?"

She nodded, staring straight ahead as if seeing into the future.

CHAPTER 15 - FAREWELL TO SMITHSON

Jacob Barron did not die the night of his accident, nor the next day while his father had been intent on harming Stevie Vegas. He slipped into a coma when ambulance officers arrived and was transported on the critical list to Smithson General. Within the month he was taken off the critical list but remained, nevertheless, in a coma.

When Stevie's mother came to pick him up from Skateopia that night she immediately presumed the flashing lights of the ambulance were for her son, given the events of the past few weeks. When Jem came home from hospital they had a family conference on whether they should continue to make Smithson their home. All agreed, even Alexander Vegas that they should move back to Valley Dale.

After the day in the forest, Stevie never saw Chris Barron again - only his black Mercedes driving quickly by the bungalow enroute to the hospital.

The police investigated the accident at Skateopia but found Jacob Barron fell by his own hands and that no foul play was evident. They questioned Stevie briefly and cautioned him on the dangers of duels, but skating wasn't illegal and Tom Lee and his friends at Smithson High told a story of Jacob Barron pushing his luck during his last trick. The police had no alternative but to close the file, despite Chris Barron's protests no doubt.

Stevie suspected that Aunt Bessie had also spoken to his parents about the good sense of moving back to Valley Dale, given Jem and Jacob's accident. She was, Stevie thought, very persuasive.

She stayed on until they were just about ready to leave Smithson. They were to move back to their old house in Valley Dale which, interestingly, had failed to sell. The locum vets who replaced his parents at the vet clinic decided

Valley Dale did not suite them after all and preferred the larger animals usually associated with an inland practice. So after barely three months at Smithson, the Vegas family began packing to go home.

Jem's leg healed slowly and he was to be in a caste for most of the summer holidays. Stevie had already written plenty of messages on his caste from: "You'll hit 'em out of the ballpark yet", referring to Jem's baseball prowess, to "Never far away, yours Bro".

Once he learned they were leaving Smithson, Jem's happy nature returned and he was more like the Jem of old. Those last weeks and days in Smithson as a relieved Vegas family packed up their belongings, were some of the happiest family times in months.

Stevie also had more than enough time to continue his relentless questioning of Aunt Bessie on all things remotely connected to Illuminators and Shadowcasters. On their last night at Smithson Stevie asked if his aunt felt up to a walk by the river. Aunt Bessie agreed, relieved, Stevie thought, to be getting out of packing up the last of the kitchen utensils.

"You two go ahead," Sylvia Vegas said, laughing at their lame offers of further assistance. They would surely stay and help if need be. "A walk will do you both good and, anyway, Alexander has offered to help," she countered.

Mr Vegas began to protest half-heartedly. "But I packed up the saucepans before tea..."

"And you will continue to pack up the utensil draw after tea," she said, throwing a dishcloth at her husband which landed squarely on his cheek.

Between mouthfuls of his mum's chocolate cake, Jem laughed at the sight of his father with a dishcloth dripping down one cheek.

Stevie glanced at his aunt and she knew what he was thinking - the dark shadows that had fallen over the Vegas family were disappearing and each member of the family was beginning to think that life would get back to normal very soon.

As they walked down to the river, Stevie thought about Jacob Barron. His Aunt Bessie, like always, read his mind. "You know Stevie it wasn't your fault."

Stevie shrugged, not really convinced despite the reassurance. He had been preoccupied with the image of Barron as he lay lifeless at the foot of the skate ramp and it was something he could not shake.

"I'm not so sure. If I hadn't stood up to Barron, if I had of walked away, he might not be in the mess he's in now."

They reached the edge of the river, not far from the place a month ago where they had rowed out to rid the world of the Barron's cursed stone. His aunt sat down on a nearby log, while Stevie searched for flat stones to skim across the water's edge. Finding a handful of perfect ones, he expertly began to send them jumping across the river.

His aunt continued. "Stevie we all choose our own path. You know that because that night you chose your own. What did Chipara say to you...here at this very place...not so long ago? He said you would need to learn to use your power wisely and you did. You did not use it against Jacob Barron. Even though you could have caused his fall, just as he caused your own, you didn't, did you?"

Stevie stopped sending his stones flying for a minute and turned back to answer his aunt. "No...I didn't."

"And what did you learn that night. What lesson has stayed with you?" his aunt pressed on.

He thought for a long time before answering. "That no power is worth having if you have to become corrupt to keep it. And you've got to stand up for yourself and what you think is right because if no-one does then people like the Shadowcasters will triumph."

His aunt smiled knowingly. "That my boy is why you carry the mark of an Illuminator. Don't ever forget that the brightness of a star can become a guide on the darkest of nights."

Stevie sat down then, next to his aunt, satisfied with his conscience and together they watched the sun set behind the far off hills.

EPILOGUE

The Vegas family couldn't leave Smithson soon enough. Under Chris Barron's influence the town blamed them for Jacob Barron's accident. But once they were on the road and Smithson receded into the distance, like a bad dream becoming a distant memory they relaxed and even dared to hope life would be better back in Valley Dale.

And it was.

The Vegas boys settled happily and quickly back into Valley Dale life. Stevie was allowed to ride his skateboard to and from school and soon perfected a double 360 at the local skate park. It was far less grand when compared to Smithson's Skateopia, but his old skate park was what he knew and loved. The half-pipes, grind rails and jumps were quite enough to keep Stevie challenged and he decided to enter the Regional's that first year back.

Before long Jem was even back on at the baseball park with all the skill and agility befitting Valley Dale's Under 11 leadoff hitter. His slight limp from his fall was only barely noticeable and didn't hold him back in the slightest. They even gave him a "runner" to run for him between bases that first season. Skating wasn't the only Regional competition the Vegas' attended that year and Jem was awarded Man of the Match, scoring a home run against a very good ball.

Mr and Mrs Vegas resumed their veterinarian practice and soon life returned to normal. The Vegas boys even made a run through McShady's motor wrecking yard one night for old time's sake.

Stevie and Jem re-enrolled at Valley Dale High and were glad to be back among friends. As for the inevitable bullies that exist in any schoolyard, the Vegas boys were more than a match for them after dealing with the likes of Jacob Barron and McCauley.

The beginning of the school term heralded a new start and Stevie looked forward not backwards as he made his way to his classroom. Taking a seat next to the window he looked around the room. A young girl he had not seen before was making her way through the rows of desks to the empty seat beside him. She sat down and Stevie introduced himself.

"Hi, I'm Stevie Vegas."

She turned shyly to him. "I'm Mary Lou Nova. What did you say your last name was again?"

"Vegas. Why?"

"Just a hunch, but you wouldn't be related to Bessie Orion by any chance? She said she had a nephew named Stevie."

Stevie smiled at the new girl. "That's my Aunt Bessie for sure. How do you know her?"

"I know your Aunt Bessie quite well. She once helped me out...well, actually, more than helped me out...she saved my life."

Stevie was about to question the strange girl further, but no sooner had he opened his mouth than she was off, calling over her shoulder: "Nice to meet you Stevie Vegas. I hope we can be friends."

Stevie, although slightly puzzled by the Aunt Bessie connection, returned the girl's smile for the time being. He was thinking he should catch up with her again at recess when something caught his attention outside and he glanced out the window, watching the crowds of students disperse to their classrooms. It was then he remembered where he had heard the name Mary Lou. She had been the young girl Aunt Bessie saved from an oncoming car. He looked across the room and saw she was talking animatedly to Taylor Simpson.

Never mind, he had plenty of time to catch up with her later. He turned back to the window, noticing the schoolyard was empty now. A small West wind was picking up the leaves and blowing them in circles. Stevie looked up at the clearness of the blue sky which wasn't forecasting storms yet, though he could feel a storm approaching. Puzzling.

The wind picked up its pace and a vague rustling, whistling sound played at the edges of Stevie's earshot. It was almost as if the West wind, which had travelled from the inland, carried a whisper of things to come. He cocked his head to one side to pick up the vague sounds in the wind that he knew were meant for him.

It was Jacob Barron's voice he heard in that moment, saying that he and others were coming for him and would not fail this time.

Startled, Stevie looked around the classroom, wondering if anyone else could hear Jacob's threats. He felt conscious of Mary Lou's attention focused on him. He turned to her and their eyes locked. Stevie knew instinctively she, somehow, understood.

They nodded silently to one another, as if reading each other's thoughts.

About the Author:

M.R. Weston (Maryann Weston) is a professional writer, training initially as a journalist and editor. She grew up on a farm in Australia and learnt early that the best adventures in life are the ones you seek out and follow.

She has made it her mission to follow her dreams, including writing novels, and has combined her love of adventure and new horizons with a vivid imagination and ability to tell a good story.

Maryann has a Bachelor of Communications (Journalism) and is also a qualified teacher and counselor, with a Graduate Diploma in Education and a Diploma of Community Services.

She currently works as a journalist, editor and public relations professional and is a mum to three boys. She lives with her family in rural NSW, Australia.

About the Shadowscape Trilogy:

Shadowscape - The Stevie Vegas Chronicles is the first book in a trilogy. The second novel is Dawn of the Shadowcasters published by Lodestone Books in 2014.

Maryann will be working on the final book in the trilogy, Luminous, in 2014-2015.

You can follow Maryann's blog at http://extrasensitiveperson.wordpress.com/ or follow her on Twitter @MaryannWeston.